LOST BUT NOT FORGOTTEN

A Story of Redemption During the Great Tribulation

A NOVEL

SKYE BURGDORF

Lost But Not Forgotten

A Story of Redemption During the Great Tribulation

By Skye Burgdorf

Because of the dynamic nature of the Internet, any web addresses or links contained in this book may have changed since publication and may no longer be valid.

Paperback ISBN-13: 979-8-9871672-0-5

Published in the United States of America.

Dedication

To those lost but not forgotten. Seek the Kingdom of God.

What People Are Saying

"God is using Skye Burgdorf to bring a message of hope to people who are very close to committing their lives to the Lord. Every Christian should leave multiple copies of this book in strategic places in your home, your relatives' homes, and your business. This book will bring hope, healing, and heaven to those who may be lost but are not forgotten. I love this book. Please read it."

~Troy Waugh, Author/Mentor and coach to Christian leaders

"Have you ever wondered what life after the rapture will be like for those who aren't yet fully committed believers? This book immerses the reader into the world after the rapture and creates food for thought for believers and nonbelievers alike. This is a wonderful story of God's amazing grace."

~Charity Kimes, Author/Speaker

"A fantastic read, *Lost But Not Forgotten* held my attention from page 1! Hard to put down, you'll love the character development and story that takes place. A true page-turner, this is a must-read!"

~Amanda Mason, Author

Epigraph

Matthew 24: 21-22 (New King James Version)

> "For then there will be great tribulation, such as has not been since the beginning of the world until this time, no, nor ever shall be. And unless those days were shortened, no flesh would be saved; but for the elect's sake those days will be shortened."

Table of Contents

Part 2-Mid-Tribulation

Part 3-Nearing the End of the Tribulation

Acknowledgements

This book has been a two-year process with life happening in between. It's been hard to keep motivation at times, but I knew I was supposed to write this book. My husband and my kids have allowed me to be buried in my work for this book for countless hours. They have encouraged me and been excited to one day read it.

My husband Chris, you have built me cozy fires on autumn nights, made me tea, and lifted the windows with a blanket for me when the rain was coming down. Anything to help me write and I'm truly grateful. You have also helped me in knowledge in certain areas when it comes to scripture and guns. I know that's rather a funny thing to say but once a Marine, always a Marine. So, thank you "Preacher Man."

I want to thank my mom and dad for giving me the childhood and memories to look back on to be able to write this book. My senses of farm life were in full force. Mom, we are so much alike, and you poured your thoughts and soul into me as well. Many times, I asked you for advice and you helped me in my brainstorming. You were excited to see what else I would bring into the book, and you could also see parts of my life in this book. You helped me make this book possible. Thank you so much for believing in this story. I always felt that if I was raptured right now, I would want something on my kitchen table to point people to Christ.

Dad, I love how you wanted mom to continue reading my book on the way to Florida, not knowing it was me who wrote it! That motivated me and made me feel like I could keep going.

My Gran (Doris Hargrove), thank you for giving me advice, for reading my rough, rough draft, and for encouraging me to not take the "sexy" out of the book. It was hard for me, but you continued to tell me that "Whoever is left will still be human, and they would be looking for companionship." At times we can be too stuffy, but God already knows our every thought. You truly have always been there for me. Thank you.

My brother (Heith Woodard), you allowed me to call you crying many times when I was green to researching about the rapture. You knew that my heart was in a very serious spot, but you stayed on the phone with me and really just let me cry. That's what brothers are for, and I love you.

Mrs. Susan Hill, you and Pastor Lynn have been such mentors to Chris and me. We admire your commitment to Christ and have learned that your quietness at times is such a powerful tool. I have tried to be quiet and listen more.

Pastor, Chris has been in unity with me in this book, and I know you have talked with him about always being in unity and supportive.

Whitney Johnson, you have been there through my thoughts, willing to read my drafts, talking with me about end time events. We have homeschooled our child-ren seeing the ways of the world, and you have helped me move my hair salon. You have the gift of making me laugh and are always encouraging. I appreciate you letting me see you as one of the characters in this book. Thank you for taking the time and writing my foreword. You are such a talented writer and I love how when you do something you put your whole heart into it.

Thank you to my editor, Betty Norlin. You have worked alongside me helping me get my book out to readers truly the way I wanted it. You have given me motivation to carry it out, and you would remind me when I would get frustrated the real reason I was doing this. Thank you for all of your endless hard work on this.

Disclaimer

Please know that this book is a work of fiction. There are questions that many of us have, and this should cause us to want to dig into the Word of God. We need to find truth and we will only get that from His Word. The purpose of this book is to help people ponder their salvation. I personally believe that young children are innocent until they can fully understand that Jesus Christ died on the cross for their sins. Some questions seem impossible for us to answer such as: will there be children after the rapture? I believe only God can know this. We can form our own opinions, but we cannot be certain. For the sake of the story and to bring things to life for you, the reader, I will let you ponder on this issue. More than any of these questions; I hope that you ask yourself, "Who is my Savior?"

Foreword

It is with the greatest honor, privilege, and joy that I get to introduce to you Skye Burgdorf. Since Elementary School I have had the opportunity to create memories with her that will outlive our time on this earth. From an early age Skye was the girl that glowed. The girl you wanted to know. The girl you wanted to understand.

That glow that attracted you like a magnet was her deep love of Christ, as you would soon learn upon getting to know her. Always sweet natured and coupled with her fierce faith became a catalyst for so many of us in our small town, to pick up a Bible, and to go to the Lord with that same uncompromising love of His Word she consistently alluded to.

Skye was my calm, and I was her storm. We have walked through life's toughest times together. If our friendship was a sound, it would undoubtedly be laughter.

For years upon years, we have talked for hours about our faith in Jesus and our excitement of his imminent return. Over hot cups of coffee snuggled in blankets, over the phone with our kids squealing in the background, over lunches, dinners, playdates, and all in between.

It came as no surprise to me when years ago she revealed she was writing a book about the rapture. My excitement was raw and riveting! I knew it was God ordained and He would speak through her vicariously within the ink of each page.

Within this warm and compelling story, you will find yourself enthralled and enchanted by each character. Falling in love with each of them and excitedly hoping upon hope they find true salvation in the only One who can save us.

Skye Burgdorf

A story full of suspense that will have you anxious to finish chapter after chapter. Emotional highs and lows as the story carries you from the rapture through the trials of the tribulation.

Friendship, family, and love abound as the story reveals our critical and indisputable need for Christ Jesus on this side of Heaven. And the vital importance of spreading the Gospel in preparation of His return.

The Bible relentlessly tells us not to fear, for Jesus is our joy. Congruently it expresses the great need for us to be prepared at all times even though we know not the day nor hour He will come for us. Mark 13:32-37 (NKJV) says "But of that day and hour no one knows, not even the angels in heaven, nor the Son, but only the Father. Take heed, watch, and pray; for you do not know when the time is. *It is* like a man going to a far country who left his house and gave authority to his servants, and to each his work, and commanded the doorkeeper to watch. Watch therefore, for you do not know when the master of the house is coming—in the evening, at midnight, at the crowing of the rooster, or in the morning—lest, coming suddenly, he finds you sleeping. And what I say to you, I say to all: WATCH!"

My hope for each reader: The unbeliever—it ignites a fire within you to want to come to know Jesus, the Father, and fall in love with Him. To discover His plans for you and immerse yourself within the pages of His good book, the Bible, before it's too late. For believers—my hope is you feel excited in your salvation and gain urgency in your spirit after reading this book to be prepared! And prepare those around you by speaking truth and sharing the gospel. So, no one we know, and love, will be lost.

Whitney Johnson

Introduction

The Jewish Wedding

The groom "Hatan" and the bride "Kalah" have their families at the city gates. He offers her a drink of wine from his cup. She accepts and takes a drink in front of her family. This is their commitment for betrothal. Not knowing the day or hour her groom will come, only Hatan's father knows, and is the one to send the groom.

Hatan then has a year to prepare. He leaves excited, ready to build onto his father's house. Kalah prepares herself for her groom, wanting everything to be perfect. To prepare for her dress she visits city merchants, looking for the perfect material, lace, and jewels.

As the date gets closer to a full year Hatan's groomsmen are near, ready for the father's announcement: "It is time for Hatan to claim his bride."

Kalah is nearby knowing that the season for her wedding is close, but not knowing the exact day or hour. Her bridesmaids are nearby and Kalah sleeps in her wedding dress every night until her groom and his groomsmen come.

One of the groomsmen blows the shofar, alerting the people who have been waiting and ready to be a part of the wedding. They gather together and parade throughout the city towards the bride. Kalah is now waiting after hearing the trumpet blow. A litter (palanquin) is laid on the ground in front of her and she respectfully steps in. They lift her up off the ground and carry her back to the father's house. Everyone who was prepared and ready for the wedding goes into the father's house. The door is then shut, and they feast at the wedding for seven days and no one is allowed to enter.

This tradition of the Galilean wedding reflects the rapture, the calling up, or the Hebrew word "Harpzo." In scripture Christ calls His followers His bride. I look forward to being called up with Jesus and having the wedding feast, seeing my brothers and sisters in Christ, and enjoying it together as a family.

My heart has felt Christ's return is imminent and we should prepare ourselves as a bride prepares for her groom.

Revelation 19:7&9a (NKJV)

"Let us be glad and rejoice and give Him glory, for the marriage of the Lamb has come, and His wife has made herself ready."

"Blessed *are* those who are called to the marriage supper of the Lamb!"

Prologue

"Mom, I hear you. I understand. Okay, well, okay, I'm pulling in the driveway." Savy got out of her shiny new car, that was now a little dusty from driving out to a sleepy little Mayberry town called Leiper's Fork, Tennessee. She was trying to grab her bags out and struggled a bit. She was not a light packer. Her mom ran out to meet her and wrapped her arms around her. "Mom, what are you wearing?" Savy said, trying not to giggle. "These are my paint clothes, don't pay any attention, this is old paint," she answered hugging her daughter tightly. Savy laughed and breathed in her mother's aroma of fresh cotton.

As she again struggled to get her bags out, her older brother came out of the house with his cowboy boots on and half his pant legs in them. "Thanks," she said exhaling. He looked up at her and smiled. "Hey sis, ain't nothin' but a thang," he said carrying in her luggage. "Watch out for that chicken mess," he said chuckling. She slapped him on the arm and followed him inside.

"So, Savy said she would come to church Sunday. We can have dinner after. Does that sound nice?" Carma said as she went back to putting her finishing touches on a table she was painting. "That sounds good to me," Savy's brother replied. "Mom, I do have to head back to New York Tuesday." "I thought we got the whole week with you," Carma said disappointed. "I wish, but I'll be here five days. Almost a week, mom." "Well, I guess I will take whatever I can get."

Her dad walked in through the backdoor. "Hello darlin'," he said, hugging her. "I think you have grown since I last saw you." "Dad, I think I'm through growing," Savy laughed as she took off her heels.

Part 1 –

After the Rapture

1 Thessalonians 4:17 (NKJV)

Then we who are *alive* and remain shall be caught up together with them in the clouds to meet the Lord in the air. And thus, we shall always be with the Lord.

2 Thessalonians 2:6-7 (NKJV)

And now you know what is restraining, that he may be revealed in his own time. For the mystery of lawlessness is already at work; only He who now restrains *will do so* until He is taken out of the way.

Matthew 24:12-13 (NKJV)

"And because lawlessness will abound, the love of many will grow cold. But he who endures to the end shall be saved."

Chapter 1

I felt my head spinning. There was a wave of guilt or a sickness that filled my insides. I never thought this would happen. *I had heard about it for years from the pulpit and didn't understand it. I thought this was just a myth. How was I not taken? Where did everybody go?* There have been reports about possible government control or alien invasion. *Then I would still be believing a lie. Wouldn't I? I mean, an alien invasion is such a far-fetched idea. I remember my family talking about prophecy, and I would shrug it off as not tangible or some sort of conspiracy.* Chaos was literally in the streets! I saw cars that had rammed into the sides of buildings, people yelling, screaming, and smashing windows to take advantage of the chaos. *I didn't know what was happening, but I needed to find out.*

I thought my mom had lost her marbles when I was a teenager. So many times, I would try to tell her to stop worrying about me. I didn't need prayer. I was fine! She would call me many times and tell me how bad the world was and how she just wanted me to go to church with her. So, I would, a few times here and there, just to make her happy, but I didn't need to. I felt my book of business had taken off, and I didn't need the extra stress of taking time out of my week and going to church. I believed Jesus existed, but I was unsure He was the son of God. I'd read about great men of history. I thought he must've been a great humble man. *Thinking back, though, I wonder, could my mom have been right? Was He the Savior?*

As I was driving, I couldn't help but notice an older lady lying on the pavement. I quickly pulled my car into the parking lot to help her. I put my car in park and got out to help her up and, in a panic, she was looking desperately for her son, who she couldn't find. She was able to tell me that he would always take her to the grocery store because she couldn't drive herself. She told me, "I opened a carton of eggs to check for cracks and was putting them in the buggy. I looked around to see where my son had gone, and he was nowhere in sight! I looked all over the store, scared for his life. My eyes darted as I swiftly walked looking down each aisle. I felt like my heart was beating out of my chest and a sick feeling came over me as I looked at the meat counter, the deli, down the bread aisle, and then back to the checkout. I could hear the screaming and crying. I felt as if I could loudly wail out of fear myself. 'Seth!' I began to scream. My eyes felt flooded and hot. Abandoning my buggy, I stumbled trying not to trip over my own two feet. I felt as if I was in a bad nightmare and needed to pinch myself awake. When I got outside the pavement sucked me in, causing me to fall and scrape my knee," she said, realizing what she was recalling was all too real.

She needed to get to her son, Seth's, car. She said she felt as if she was being pulled to it as she went outside, almost as if something or someone had taken control of her, yet she could still feel her leg throbbing from the pain. "Seth! No! He wasn't there! What happened!?" She looked around; and could hear the shrill honking of cars, screeching as one of the cars darted into the Goodwill. Glass exploding as it continued to run without a driver. I thought about what she had told me. "It is hell on earth!" I knew I couldn't leave her there, and after a while, she accepted my offer to give her a ride home.

When we stopped for gas, I noticed a big burly farmer, dressed in faded blue jeans and dusty boots, pumping gas next to us. He had one tear stream down his face. He wiped it away from his eye so no one would see, but his tear left a trail down his dirty face. His face looked kind, and his heart looked lost. He looked to be about sixty years old. I watched as I saw him go to grab something under his seat. Suddenly, a man pointed a gun right at me. I gasped and held up my hands. Then the farmer held a gun to his back, and demanded, "Drop the gun! I suggest you step back, or I will pull the trigger," the farmer said not letting the guy out of his sight. I began crying and grabbed the hand of the lady I was driving home, Ms. Lou. She looked shocked and relieved all at the same time. Farmer Henry grabbed the gun the man had dropped that was lying on the ground and put it behind his back and the other one in his holster.

After I calmed my nerves a bit, I spoke up, "Sir, would you tell us your story?" He replied, "Welp, all I know is my wife was right about everythin'. She tried and tried to get me to go to church. I wouldn't listen. I had too many other things to do 'round the farm. Somethin' always needed fixin', or cows needed milkin', animals needed to be fed. I always had an excuse. She would just look at me and say, 'Well, I'm goin' without ya then!'" He looked at me with his lips quivering. "You see," he said, "I never accepted Jesus as my Lord and Savior. I'd heard my wife talk about it more than once, and now I'm left without her. If it's anythin' like she says it's gonna be, we have got to be ready."

I asked him where they were and how it had happened to him. He told us they were in the truck on the way home from town. She needed new shoes for work. "I was drivin', and we had just gotten ice cream. Her favorite was mint chocolate chip. She was laughin' at me, crackin' a joke, and mid laughter I looked over, and her weddin' rings were lying there. I swerved off the road and felt like I had a heart attack. Right there, I began prayin' for the first time."

I started thinking to myself, *if this was the rapture...what are we supposed to do? What else is about to happen? Why would an excellent loving God do this to anybody? We have no one. We have just been forgotten about. I can't imagine burning in Hell if this is my destiny.* After talking to the sweet frail old lady, Ms. Lou, who I dropped off at her house after the gas station, and the big, burly, tough and tender farmer, Henry, I tossed and turned all night long.

It's been three days and I haven't even shown up for work since all this happened. I don't even know how to go about everyday life anymore.

My somewhat "boyfriend" Nick didn't understand what I was going through. It's like he was oblivious. He kept telling me to chill out, but I lost it with him. How could I not? How did he not even see the pain everyone, including me, was going through? He seemed just to be going along and feeding into some of the most insane stories the media was feeding everyone. They said they wanted to make sure they don't lose anybody else. He was always telling me their next update.

Yesterday afternoon, we went for a walk to try and figure out what we should do. I had tried to call my parents every night since, but nothing. I got so distressed with him because he kept changing the subject and telling me that I was hyperfocused and irrational. I just told him, "Leave!" I began walking faster than him, slamming every door I could as I entered the lobby of my apartment building and went through the hallway toward our place. As soon as I got home, I began packing his things for him. I told him, "I am being irrational, and you need to leave now." He honestly didn't seem too upset, because maybe I had just over-focused on this. Perhaps I was being unreasonable, but I couldn't help but think he was the one being irrational.

How dare he does not want to argue back and try to unpack his things! How dare he just be okay with it all. Did he even love me? Was he just here as someone to help pay for a place to stay? Did he even have a true heart? A soul even? He just left when I handed him his packed bags. I couldn't believe it.

When I went to bed that night, I tossed and turned, tossed and turned, tossed and turned. Okay, counting sheep…no, that never worked. I got up, warmed up some hot chamomile tea on the stove, and turned on some *Friends*. Background noise usually puts me at ease. Sometimes I felt like I could go all day long in circles, and at the end of the day, I needed laughter in the background.

It's now been four days after the chaos, and as the sunlight glowed through my window, I could see the dust sparkling in the rays that were dancing through the apartment. I stretched and wiped my eyes as I went to make my first cup of coffee. My friend Jules, who also lived in New York, and worked as a hair stylist, was banging on my door.

She had made the drive back from a hair show in Boston, Massachusetts. "I'm coming!" She walked in with more energy than I could muster as I opened the door. "Okay! Look at this!" As she pulled up an article on her phone. I grabbed her and hugged her immediately. "I'm so glad you made it back. I was so worried." "Look, Savy! I told you they were going to be doing this next! Look at all these bigger cities putting embedded chips in people's hands! And people are actually going along with this!" I looked at her with wonder as

I was still trying to wake up and sip my coffee. She kept going.

"My sister Kim told me this was coming! I never believed her. At the time, I didn't see the big deal with it. I mean, honestly, look at technology right now! We can't even sweep our floors or wipe our butts without having some sort of technology!" She kept going without even taking a breath, and I could barely keep up! How on earth can she talk that fast? She must've had four cups of coffee so far, and I'm just on my first.

"Savy! Savy!? Are you listening to me?" I took a deep breath, "Yes! I'm sorry. Yes!" Jules continued, "Okay, Savy. I think we need to get away. Go somewhere." I held up my hand holding onto my coffee, still in my slouchy pajamas and my hair in a messy bun. "Jules, it's been days since I've even stepped foot in my office. They may fire me. I stayed up all night trying to call mom and dad, no answer. I tried calling my brother to see if he knew anything, but he didn't answer either. I'm worried they are gone."

"Savy," Jules began again pulling the blinds up for her to look out at the city. "I don't think anybody is worried about legal documents at a time like this!" I grimaced at more light filtering in the apartment. I held up my hand to try and ward off some of the brightness. I glanced down at my phone and my boss had texted me a few minutes earlier. "Savy, we will not move forward with any of the legal documents drawn up before September 19th. No action is needed at this time." *No action is needed at this time. My world is falling apart! How in the world can I even pay for anything?*

Jules sat down next to me. "We can't stay here." She saw my swollen eyes, and she knew how close I was with my parents. Grabbing both hands, Jules looked intently at me. "Let's go home." I didn't even have to think about it. Somehow, I got a jolt of determination and immediately got up and packed my bags and grabbed three credit cards from the safe. *I never used these,* I thought. I've been a paralegal for nine years and loved my job. It was very stressful at times, but I worked hard for my job, and I had always been proud that I had made it just fine on my own. Only my world felt like it was caving in, and I had no clue how to control it. I poured another cup of coffee and we headed for Tennessee.

The only thing my friend Jules and I could think of was going back home. We drove all day and all night to our sleepy little town of Leiper's Fork, where the sun was hot, but the breeze felt so good. I felt like I could breathe a little bit. Not totally, but it was just different than the hustle and bustle of the city life I had gotten used to. Here nothing stayed open past 8:00pm, and I'm pretty sure I pulled into my parents' driveway on fumes. I had dropped Jules off at her sister's old house first. I just honestly needed some time to think by myself. I stepped out and could smell farm life. My heels dug into the soggy ground as I tried to get my bag out of the trunk.

I walked up the creaky steps to the front porch. I tried to find my key in the dark. I finally got inside and turned on the light. I broke down and just began to cry. I couldn't hold it in any longer. Tears came pouring down my face. I tried to take deep breaths, but the more I tried to breathe, the faster the tears poured. I couldn't stop. I sat down on the steps inside that led up to my old bedroom with my head in my hands and kept crying.

As I finally looked up, I saw this blessing over the door. I remembered my mom talking about it being some sort of Jewish blessing or something. I just stared at it and started talking to God. Maybe I was feeling mad. I had been so numb since all this started less than a week ago; I didn't really even know what I was feeling. *"God, why would you leave me? Why? Why do I feel so lost? You took everything! My mom was the one I called for anything. I can't do this without my parents! I don't understand! I don't understand! Do you hear me? Are you even listening to me? Are you there? Nobody else is here, are you?!"*

I got up and started walking around the house and thinking if there was anything that would maybe strike a memory, a conversation, or anything. I saw my dad's old spurs and thought back to the time he taught me how to ride and all the rides we did together.

I may have been in the city for too long, but I could sure remember the feeling of riding in a big open field. Daddy listened to all my stories as I talked a million miles a minute and he always called me his little girl. It felt cold in the house, so I started a fire in the fireplace. As the house was just getting warmed up, I went to take a bath. They had an old clawfoot bathtub, and I just relaxed and laid my head back. It was so quiet, but I could hear the frogs chirping outside. It was beginning to feel like fall out. Still sunny and warm during the day but very cool at night. My favorite season. Brightly colored leaves and the crispness of the air, my brother and I used to jump in them when we were kids. Every year we would have bonfires, roast marshmallows, and cook hot dogs.

What an awesome childhood we had. He played football for a small school right outside of Leiper's Fork. I sat in the warm bath and thought about those late nights under the stars, hearing the band play and watching football under the bright lights. He was a believer and prayed before every game. He would always look at me and say, "Saf! Watch the whole game! God is with us!" I was there every Friday night cheering the Jackets on with pride. "That's my brother!" I would yell. Our family was always close. They were there no matter what.

Why didn't I listen? I slid down into the water feeling the water rush over my head, holding my breath. *If I could only have one more day with them. Just one, God.* I came up out of the water, with my eyes closed just thinking of the many memories I shared with my parents and how they always took time for us. Mom tried to get me to church, but I was so rebellious in my teenage years, and I just wanted to go off and make it on my own. I didn't want anything to do with this little town. Now I'm thinking it may not have been so bad. A little quiet can do a lot after hearing everyone else's problems. Right now, I have my own issues I have to figure out. Jules had been right. We need to lay low for a while and figure out what's next.

When I heard that crazy rooster crow, I rolled right out of bed, almost crashing onto the floor!! *What the heck? It's only 5:00 am! How did they ever sleep with that thing?* I grabbed my robe out of my bag to see if they had any coffee to be made. I got the coffee started when I heard a knock at the door. "What? Who? Uggghhh!" I stomped to the door and saw a man about my age...a rather handsome country boy. "Just a sec!!!" I ran into the bathroom and looked in the mirror. My eyes were very swollen from crying the night before. "Oh great!" I splashed water on my face and smeared the foundation on quickly. I ran back to the door and opened the door with my arms crossed. "I'm sorry, can I help you at 5:30 this morning!?"

He turned from petting our old dog Leroy and gave a little smirk. "Your daddy was a good man." I looked at him with my brows furrowed a bit, wrapping my robe tightly around me. "Yes, he was, and thank you." "I come by and feed the dog and chickens since all this has happened. I kind of wondered if you were gonna come home. He talked about you a lot. He was a godly man and always invited me to church with him, but church wasn't my thing."

I looked, trying to understand. "You have been taking care of the animals for my dad?" "Yes, ma'am." "Oh, well, thank you..." "Tucker." I gave a little smile, "Thank you, Tucker." "No problem, ma'am. I will just leave the eggs in the basket on the porch for you." "Oh, okay, thank you." I shut the door. *Tucker...*I thought. I went to make my coffee and started rummaging through things trying to find pictures. I stumbled across some pictures of me, my brother, mom, and dad. Some images of mom and dad and their hippie days, wedding pictures, some of my grandmother, family get-togethers, creek stomping photographs, and then I found a note.

To: My Savy

If you're reading this, it's too late. I never wanted you to endure some of the things that scripture talks about. Savy, your dad and I, and your brother, are with Jesus. This was the rapture that we have tried talking about. I want you to find my Bible. I have verses highlighted for you to read. I will try to explain it as best as I can, but it is for you to live out and give yourself to Christ now. You may have to endure severe persecution. They will tell you it's for your safety and security but try to stand firm. Do not accept anything in your hand. He wants complete control of this world, and God is letting him have some power for a little while before the final battle.

I don't know everything that's going to take place, but you will not be able to buy or sell without the mark in your hand. They will want a cashless society. The best thing you can try to do is live off the grid. Stay off social media and let go of your cell phone and any electronics. I've always told you being a Christian is serious business. Well, honey, it's time to get serious. Our God is gracious. He did not take us out of spite. He gave you ample opportunity to accept Him as your Lord and Savior. Jesus is the only way. He is the Truth and the Life. No one gets to the Father except through Him. You have been living a life that's lost. I want you to know that you are lost, but you have never been forgotten. Honey, I love you so much. I love you with all of my heart. Your dad and I have been praying for the lost. That's you, Savy. You are lost and need to pray and give your life over right now.

Pray this: Lord Jesus, I can't live in this time alone without you. I'm asking that You help me to be faithful during these challenging times that I'm about to live out. Help me, Lord, to be strong. I pray for You to come into my heart, soul, and mind right now. I believe in Your mighty awesome name. Jesus, I believe that You died on the cross to cover all my sins and that You rose again. Lord Jesus, I pray that You care for me during this time. I pray for Your supernatural power and strength to be with me. In Your Holy name. AMEN.

Now Savy, I want you to know that with every ounce of my being, you will have to be willing to die for Him if they try to kill you. Stay around people who are His light. Ephesians 6:12 (NKJV) says, "For we do not wrestle against flesh and blood but against the principalities, against powers, against the rulers of the darkness of this age, against spiritual hosts of wickedness in the heavenly places." Savy, please stay strong. I have more letters hidden under the stairs.

With the most amount of

Love,

Mom

Chapter 2

After coming in from feeding the animals and doing all his chores, Henry kicked off his muck boots and warmed up by the fire. He looked at the flames as he kneeled down to put another piece of wood on the fire. He thought about the eternal death of Hell, and he was resting on his assurance that his Maggie was in Heaven. While still on his knees, he bowed his head, and prayed out loud.

"Lord Jesus, my almighty Savior, I am not worthy of bein' saved out of what's to come, but I ask if I have to endure, help me endure until the very end of my life. Thank you for savin' my sweet Mag. I am desperately sorry and again ask for your forgiveness that I didn't accept you soon enough. Help me, Lord. Just help me is all I know and all I'm askin'."

He slowly got up and went to fix something to eat. His basset hound began to howl on the porch at the coyotes nearby, and Henry scared them off by getting his shotgun and firing once off the porch. "Get on outta hea!" he said as he came back to finish frying his egg. He was flipping the egg in the skillet and could hear Mag in his ear, "Those crazy coyotes! They need to leave our Lazy Susy alone! You know the reason she starts howling is she's warning us! She knows they will get after our livestock! With that creek behind us, that's the price we pay!" Henry could imagine her wringing the dish towels out and throwing them over the sink. He took a long, deep breath.

The dishes were starting to pile up again in the sink, and Henry decided to take it upon himself to reload them into the dishwasher. He knew he didn't load the dishwasher to her standards, and if he did ever decide to help, she wouldn't say a word. She would just smile at him and be happy for the help. They often knew what each other was thinking, and sometimes they would even finish each other's sentences. Henry and Maggie were high school sweethearts. He grew up working on the farm from the time he could sling hay. They couldn't wait to get married and were wed as soon as Maggie graduated. Henry waited on Maggie to graduate for two years. He would work, and after school, Maggie would go into the old drugstore and help with the meds. She would either help count or find people's prescriptions that were ready to be picked up. If anybody had terrible health, Maggie would run it by to them on her way home. At the end of the day, Henry would wait for Mag on her parent's front porch swing and tell her good night.

He really was a simple man and married a simple wife. She never wanted to spend extra money on herself. In fact, Henry had to make her go out many times and get a new outfit. She always told him she was fine, and she would manage. She never went to get her nails done like other high-maintenance women, but she could not go without having her hair fixed up. That was maybe the one place she enjoyed going to was the beauty shop. She would come home telling of all the latest news because Mag didn't ever want to get into the other gossip going around the beauty shop. She maybe didn't state her opinions, but she sure listened and stated them to Henry when she got home. Mag didn't cover all her silver hair. She wanted to look very natural, but she would say, "I know I'm old, but I'm not that old!" So, she would have them put some kind of foils in her hair. They made her look like she was from outer space somewhere or that she was going to pick up a signal.

When Henry finished the dishes, he took a shower, put his pajamas on, and laid in bed. He looked over at his wife's Bible. She had bought him a Bible, but he didn't care to read it. He wasn't interested nor felt he could really understand it. There was something about picking up her Bible, though. She had important verses highlighted and little notes written in the margin. He missed her, and this was the closest he could get. So, he picked up her Bible. The pages were worn, and the book's spine was falling apart, but there was something so sweet about it. He held it close to his heart and began to cry. "Okay, Mag, I'm really tryin'..." "Lord, please be with me as I read Your Word. Help me to understand what I'm about to read." He opened up where he had left off the night before.

In Mark 9:14-29 (NKJV) Henry read about a boy who was being healed of demon possession. He was mute, and whenever the spirit seized him, he threw his body down, foamed at the mouth, and gnashed his teeth. They were asking Jesus to have compassion and help them. Jesus replied in verse 23, "If you can believe, all things *are* possible to him who believes." In verse 24, the boy's father immediately cried out, "Lord, I believe; help my unbelief!" In verses 25-29 Jesus rebuked the unclean spirit and commanded the spirit out. The spirit then cried out and left the boy's body, and the people thought the boy was dead. Jesus then took the boy by the hand and lifted him up. The disciples then asked Jesus why they were not able to perform this miracle and Jesus replied, "This kind can come out by nothing but prayer and fasting."

Henry gently closed the Bible and called out, "Lord Jesus, I believe. Help my unbelief." Henry set the Bible on the nightstand, cut his lamp off, and drifted off to sleep.

Henry slept well when he saw Maggie in a field full of daisies. The wind was blowing her hair. She was happy. Smiling. As she was enjoying the sunshine, she said, "Henry! Henry, God has you. You are strong, Henry. Be strong." "Maggie? Maggie." "Henry, believe."

The next morning, Henry rose early, like normal. He pulled on his coveralls and muck boots and headed to milk the cows. The cold ground crunched under his feet, and he clasped his hands, rubbing them together and blowing his warm breath in between his palms. As he was hooking the cows up to the machines, he was still so tired, and he couldn't help but think about his dream. Henry dreamed of Mag off and on. He didn't know if it was because he missed her so much or because God was trying to comfort or show him something. He bowed his head in the barn, and again prayed out loud.

"Lord, I know I'm not the best at pickin' up signals, and I sure am tryin'. I pray that you help me to believe in You. I mean, maybe I'm like the boy's father I was readin' about last night. Help my unbelief." He remembered that verse 29 mentioned fasting and prayer. "Lord, I know I'm not demon-possessed, but I'm goin' to try this fastin' and prayin' thing. I have no clue what you want from me or what I need to be doin' right now. Show me, Lord. A-Men."

Sitting in the tack room; feed, medical supplies, halters, and lead ropes surrounding him, he got up to make sure the chickens had some corn and water. When everything was finished, he went back inside and was about to fry some sausage and put biscuits in the oven, but then remembered he was supposed to be fasting. So, he poured him some coffee, took a couple of sips, and then bowed his head. When he finished his prayer, he grabbed Mag's Bible. *If Maggie knew I was doin' this, she wouldn't believe it. She would ask, "Did you eat a sausage and biscuit today...?"* The doctor often tried to get me to diet to bring down my high cholesterol. It was inevitable, though. Whenever I would cave, Mag knew it without me even admitting it to her. She would fuss at me if she found my wrappers left over from my biscuit in the truck. "Henry! The doc told you not to eat these high fatty foods! You have got to listen!" I would always reply, "Well, I haven't done that bad, you see. This is the only thin' I had for breakfast." Mag would then roll her eyes, knowing she couldn't get through to me.

I turned to the first verse I came to, which was Matthew 6:33. Mag had written at the top of her Bible, "Seek first the kingdom of God and His righteousness." As

I glanced at the entire verse, I noticed she had written besides verse 18, "fasting in secret." Verse 17 read, "But you, when you fast, anoint your head and wash your face, so that you do not appear to men to be fasting, but to your Father who *is* in the secret *place*; and your Father who sees in secret will reward you openly."

When Henry finished his prayer time, he turned on the news. They were showing New York City and how frantic everybody was. It still hadn't calmed down since everyone disappeared over a week ago. People were running around stealing and had no love at all. He nuked his coffee in the microwave. As he sipped on his coffee and watched the news, he noticed one of the news anchors mention that many police, doctors, and lawyers had stopped working altogether.

There was too much chaos even to control. *I don't like where this is goin'...* Henry thought. He thought about Savy and Ms. Lou and wondered how they were doing. Ms. Lou seemed scared to death when they talked. She had been pretty shaken and, at times, couldn't even speak. He had met them at the gas station. Savy was filling her car, and Ms. Lou was in the passenger seat. This man tried to rob Savy while she was at the pump, but Henry grabbed his gun from under his seat and threatened the man. He told him to leave Savy alone, or he would shoot. The man backed off, dropped his gun, and ran, and Henry stood there watching Ms. Lou and Savy, as she finished gassing up her car.

Ms. Lou was scared and needed a ride home, and Savy had reassured Ms. Lou that she would get her home safely. Savy knew at the time that Ms. Lou needed that reassurance. Henry walked over to Savy and Ms. Lou to see how they were, and they ended up exchanging phone numbers. He asked Ms. Lou if she was doing okay. She replied, "Umm...I...I... think so?"

Henry told Savy to please be careful and asked her to call so that he knew they arrived home okay. In the midst of Henry's own pain, he still had a heart for others. At that very moment in time, Savy needed that too. She and Henry continued to text checking in at times, and when she finally decided to make the journey to Tennessee, she let him know. Henry sent Savy a message.

Hi, Savy. Just wanted to check on you to see how you are doin'? Did you make it to Tennessee, okay? In a time when no one feels His presence, know that God is still the Savior. Have you heard from Ms. Lou?

He didn't expect Savy to respond so quickly.

I made it ok. Thanks for checking. TBH Last I checked on Ms. Lou, she was ok, but if you don't mind going by and checking in on her ASAP to see if she needs anything that would be great. Thanks, Henry, it means more than you know. We all have to help each other. Especially when we feel there is no one. TTYL

Henry Responded:

I'll visit sometime during the day tomorrow.

Savy:

TY

At times Henry felt so alone, but he knew he needed to do whatever God was leading him to do. He couldn't help but think of what Mag would be telling him every step of the way. If there was a homeless person, Maggie couldn't pass them by without giving them something. She didn't have a lot, but she would've given her last penny, and Henry knew now it was Jesus in her.

Chapter 3

The aroma of fresh bread filled Ms. Lou's house. While she waited for the bread to bake, she pulled out an old shoe box of memories from the attic. The old shoe box held all her most important memories of raising her two kids and she couldn't seem to part with this box of memories. She had other storage boxes of theirs, but this box was dear to her heart. Her daughter's ballet shoes were worn so much that the toe had a dark hole. She picked them up and felt the leather shoes. Her daughter always danced throughout the house, and she never lost that passion. It didn't matter where they seemed to go; she always seemed to do a little twirl. Jenny was tall and thin with long blonde hair. She laughed with her whole body and was filled with joy.

She picked up a picture of Seth and Jenny and thought to herself, *we were very close growing up. I regretted not being the mother I should've been for them.* She held on to her husband Jack's police badge and shined it with her shirt. *He was killed while on the job. A man walked up and pulled his gun out and shot him. I guess I never got over it. I'm not sure why God ever allowed that to happen to the perfect family that we waited to have for so long. Jack loved to joke and laugh and cut up with the kids. He cherished the times we were together as a family but had to work many hours. The kids missed him terribly, and when he was taken from us too soon, it felt like a hole in our hearts that had been hard to heal. I'm not sure mine ever healed.*

She picked up Seth's boy scout patch. What fond memories he was able to make with his dad. They went fishing and camping in the summers, but after his dad passed, he continued the tradition with his

Uncle Tommy. Tommy was the only one who could get close to them after that. *I guess he was the closest they could get to Jack.* Jack and Tommy were forced to be close and learned from each other because their dad had not been around much. He drank a lot and stayed away. So, Jack, the oldest, would wake his brother up early in the mornings before the sun was even peeking out. They would throw clothes on and grab their fishing poles and go fishing.

Ms. Lou picked up a small note that Jenny had written her in the shape of a heart that said, I LOVE YOU TO THE MOON AND BACK, MOMMY! *That day Jenny had spilled cereal and milk all over the floor, and I fussed at Jenny and told her to clean every bit of it up by herself. Not a moment I'm very proud of. I was tired and had just gotten in from working all day at the grocery store. She cleaned it up and left this note on my pillow. After finding it, I walked into her room, kissed her head, and apologized for being so hard on her. Some nights I would get her out of bed, show her the moon, and say, "I love you to the moon and back!"*

She picked up Seth's class ring that was blue and had his football emblem on it. He loved playing in school and had his first serious girlfriend, Angie. They were your typical couple. Seth was captain of the football team, and she was a cheerleader. It was Friday night lights, and Uncle Tommy never missed a game. *On the other hand, crowds always bothered me. I remember making some of the games and missing others.* She found Jenny's old cross necklace in the box. *As I hold it in my hand now, I honestly had forgotten about this necklace.* She took it out and put it around her neck.

Ms. Lou remembered how Seth had given that to Jenny one Christmas. *She had just had a bad breakup with her boyfriend. She cried for days off and on. Seth kept trying to figure out what to get his sister, and finally, he and Tommy walked into the house with the prettiest rose gold cross necklace. He had put so much thought into her present that year.*

She remembered it so well. *He walked into her room on Christmas Eve and told her he wasn't worth all the tears she was crying. She looked up at him, and Seth wiped a tear away from her cheek. He said, "You're my favorite sister in the whole world!" She replied, "Seth...I'm your only sister!" He smarted off, "Exactly! That's why you're my favorite!" She smacked his arm and started laughing. "Shut up!" He pulled out a rectangular box. "What's this?" she asked. He replied, "Someone who watches and knows every tear you cry. You're my best friend, Jenny." Jenny hugged his neck and replied, "You're my best friend too, Seth," and continued to ugly cry.*

She closed the box and put it on the closet shelf. Just then, the doorbell rang, and her little Pomeranian began to yip at the person at the door. "Just a second." Lou peeked around the corner to look at the front door. The front door glass was an old cut-out pattern, but it looked like a man was standing there. When Ms. Lou hesitated, he called out, "Ms. Lou, it's Henry from the night at the gas station!

Savy wanted me to come by and check on you." Ms. Lou made her way to the front door trying to calm her little dog, Mini, down.

She cracked open the front door, looking unsure of letting him inside. Henry looked at her, "Ma'am, I'm not tryin' to scare you. I don't know if you remember me, but I'm Hen..." Before he could get another word out, Ms. Lou replied, "Yes, I remember who you are." She stepped out onto the porch and sat in her smoking chair. As she pulled out a pack of Virginia Slims and a lighter from the pocket of her robe, she looked at Henry with her brows furrowed. "Would you like one?" "No. No, ma'am, I quit a long time ago." Henry used to smoke outside while farming, but Mag always fussed if she could smell smoke on his clothes. Finally, he did stop smoking, and Mag would flip if she knew he'd accepted a cigarette after working so hard at quitting. Ms. Lou lit up her cigarette, taking in that first puff and holding it in till the smoke began to leave her nostrils. Her eyes glinted at Henry, and her little Mini jumped up in her lap. "Well, actually, I had stopped smoking completely, but after all the chaos, I started back up again."

Henry played with the galluses on his overalls. Mini was still unsure of him, barking now and then. "I checked on Savy last night. I sent her a message. She was concerned about you. How you been holdin' up all by yourself?" Ms. Lou responded, "Well, my nephew has called to check on me. He has also been pretty upset. His father and mother disappeared. He now believes everything his mom and dad tried telling him. They tried telling me, but I'm just not sure I believe all that! I mean, God hasn't ever cared for me. Everything in my life has always felt upside down."

Henry looked up easy at Ms. Lou. He knew there was a lot of hurt in her voice, so he was careful not to judge. Henry couldn't judge anybody for the way they had lived. He hadn't listened either. "Well, all I can do is try to give you peace of mind. I've been diggin' into prayer and my Bible. One verse that sticks out to me that

I've been prayin' on is Lord help my unbelief. You must know that we have to allow God to start somewhere." Mini jumped down, sniffing Henry's legs. She must've smelled Lazy Susy or the farm animals on him. Ms. Lou finished up her cigarette and put it out in a bowl next to her chair. "Well, even if God did all this, I really don't understand all His reasoning." Henry replied, "Ms. Lou, I don't think we will ever know the answer to that or any other questions I have for Him."

Henry looked out at the neighborhood Ms. Lou lived in. Some people were walking their dogs. Maybe their lives didn't change like others. Maybe both partners didn't believe in Jesus. While Henry watched a couple act like normal life was to be carried on, he spoke up. "Ms. Lou, was your husband taken as well?" Ms. Lou looked up from Mini. "Not in this big disappearance, but he was taken too early from my family. He was shot while on the job by a man who held a grudge against cops. Jack was a good man. He supported our family and cared so much for us. I've never understood why this had to happen when we had a perfect life. We had two beautiful children, a house, a dog, and a good marriage. Heck, we even went to church then."

Henry let the silence dwell a little. "Well, sometimes a catastrophe like that will either draw you closer or push you further away from God. I'm guessin' by the way you're talkin', and I don't mean any disrespect at all, Ms. Lou, but it sounds like you tried givin' up on life altogether after Jack died." Henry paused, giving Ms. Lou time to receive his words. He then continued, "You see, Jesus is life and love. He is merciful, and so much more that all of us need to experience. Now, I'm not a religious person, but everythin' I've read in the Bible says that every day we are to live for Christ. The reason we were even put here on this earth is to share the gospel. Now, if we had listened to His pull on our hearts earlier and not denied His existence, we would be with Him now. I do fear and respect the Lord. I fear what we are about to have to stand against. I believe all this because I feel like there is so little love in the world anymore. When God took everybody, I believe His Spirit dwelled in them. Ms. Lou, God is love, and I believe He waited and waited on a lot of us people to accept Him, but after so many times of bein' rejected, He knew the ones that had truly made up their minds to accept Him as their Lord and Savior. Mark 13:35-36 (NKJV) says, Watch therefore, for you do not know when the master of the house is coming—in the evening, at midnight, at the crowing of the rooster, or in the morning—lest, coming suddenly, he find you sleeping."

Ms. Lou was twiddling her thumbs, looking down, "Well, I suppose your right. I did deny Him after the tragedy instead of leaning on Him. I've heard my nephew come to me worried about his talks with him and his Uncle Seth about prophecy. Seth kept trying to wake him up, trying to get him to accept Christ as his Lord and Savior. Some people will remain asleep, and he wouldn't listen because my son sounded out of his mind. I mean, everybody has said that all our lives. In and out of wars and famines, everyone thought the world was going to end. Well, I guess they were right on this one, and people were not paying attention. It's like maybe we were numb to it. The news has something bad on it every night. People just wanted to go about their everyday business. Like ignoring it or something."

Henry replied, "I think they just didn't want to pay attention and probably never believed any of this would happen. Is there anythin' I can get you? Anythin' you need right now? I know everybody needs somebody right now, and it's good to talk to someone. I don't mind if you want to come and stay with me. I have another room on the first floor of my house. I have a garden and animals to help with food."

Ms. Lou looked at Henry funny, "Henry, I appreciate your offer, but I've managed on my own just fine. I don't need anybody to keep me up." "Ms. Lou, that's not what I meant at all. Please don't misunderstand me. We are comin' into some tryin' times, and we will all need each other to pull together. This is what the church does. They pull together and help each other. Now with you livin' in this neighborhood, I would hope no one would break-in. Do you have a gun?"

"Well, yes, I do actually; it was Jack's." Henry gave her a little smirk. "Do you know how to use it?" "No, I never learned. I always made him put it in the safe as soon as he got home. Guns scared me, and I know it is the person that's shooting the gun that is scarier than the gun, but I never wanted to learn, and now that he's gone, I wish I had." "I'd love to teach you," Henry said. "Please, Ms. Lou, know that my offer always stands, and you can always change your mind and come with me if you feel safer."

"Thank you, Henry. I appreciate all that you do for people. You have a good heart, and I wonder why you weren't taken?" "There is more than just bein' a good person." "I suppose," she replied. Henry got up and shook her hand. "If my mom were here today, I would hope someone would take care of her. You have a good day and be careful. My door is always open to you, Ms. Lou." Henry got up and put his hat on. He got in his truck, looked back at Ms. Lou feeling a little worried for her, and drove off.

Ms. Lou hadn't thought about living anywhere but where she was. She looked at all her things as she stepped back inside, and thoughts came flooding into her head. *I don't know how I could ever leave all my things.* She thought about the people that had disappeared and how all their possessions were here on this earth. Her sister had told her about a scripture many times about the Lord going to prepare a mansion for her. She used to laugh and say, "Well, it's good you're getting a mansion up there because you will not have one here." Ms. Lou and her family were poor growing up, but when she married Jack, they did pretty well. Ms. Lou was proud of the life they had built together.

They tried for a long time to have kids, and then she felt a little sick one day. She came down with strep throat and could not stop vomiting. Jack decided to take her to the emergency room when she was getting too dehydrated. While they were there, she was having everything checked out, and the doctors came in and said, "Well, you have strep throat, but the fact that you're pregnant sure isn't helping." She and Jack just looked at each other in amazement. Lou was pale but smiling from ear to ear. Jack got so excited and asked the doctor if he could repeat that and confirm. The doc looked up at Jack smiling and said, "That's right, Jack, her urine sample confirmed that she is pregnant." "Wooohooo! I'm gonna be a daddy!" He walked into the hallway and started telling all the nurses at the nurse's station. "Did you happen to hear my good news? I'm going to be a father! I'm gonna be a dad!" He then called everyone he could think of from the hospital. "I've got good news he told his mother. Well, Lou is sick as a dog, but I'm going to be a dad!" Lou just laid there sick but happy. She was also amazed. She had dreamed of being a mom her whole life, but in her 40's she wasn't sure it would ever happen. From then on, they had such a wonderful family.

Jack did everything with the kids when he wasn't working. He did work a lot, but the kids' memories with him were good ones. He taught Seth how to build a fire in the wilderness. He would take Jenny out, just the two of them, for ice cream so she would know how she should be treated when she started dating. They loved their daddy so much. *The world tumbled down...and the perfect life we had...when Jack was taken from us too soon.* Life was no longer perfect...far from it.

Ms. Lou thought to herself, *I didn't do well after that. I'm sure the kids kept on going and got tired of my depressing attitude. Some days she didn't even change out of her pajamas. For a while, I had given up on life altogether. Then one day, my sister came over and ripped me a new one. She threw open the curtains and the windows. She told me to get dressed. We were leaving the house. I told her I just wanted to stay home. She used some words that shouldn't be repeated and told me to get out of bed now! So, in fear of my sister, I listened.*

She told me, "Take a shower. You stink!" After my shower, we got into her red convertible. She was always flashy and loved living life to the fullest, even if it meant having a little debt. She took me to the cemetery where Jack was buried. I looked over at her and said, "Thanks for cheering me up, sis!" She shut the car off and said get out. I got out of the car, and we walked up to his grave. My sister looked at me and said, "Sis, you have got to straighten up! Now, this is not the way to live. I know it's not what anybody wanted, but it's what we've all been dealt in this life. Jack would not want you living this way, and you know it!"

She continued to preach to me about Seth and Jenny needing their mom. From that day on, I tried to get a grip and give my kids the life they deserved and needed. It wasn't easy, and I wasn't wholly renewed, but at least I tried after that. Jack's brother, Tommy, checked in on us more than I was comfortable, but I didn't dare say anything. He did it for the kids; I knew he loved his brother. I got used to him being around, and the pain eased but didn't ever really go away. I felt I held a grudge against God. Now I am left with little to no one. My nephew Andy calls to check in on me, but Jenny, Seth, my sister, and Tommy are gone. I am lonely, but not ready to give up my home completely.

As she often did, Ms. Lou put on an old Elvis record that she and Jack used to dance to. While listening, she sliced off a piece of bread and slathered some butter on it. She rested in her rocking chair after eating. Her head went back, and she closed her eyes, trying to remember Jack, Seth, and Jenny. *Her whole life was gone, but she at least rested in the fact that if there was a God, she was sure they were there with Him. From the sounds of it, it sounded like they were right.*

Chapter 4

Savy couldn't wait to find and read the letters her mom had mentioned and found the door that went under the stairs. As she opened the door, she saw a hanging light and pulled the cord to turn it on. She immediately saw a bookshelf. There on the shelf was an old, blue, ragged, and torn around the edges, suitcase. She dusted the old suitcase off and noticed a piece of tape labeled, "Savy."

I remember this old blue suitcase, Savy thought to herself, as she began looking through everything. *It was my first suitcase when I was a little girl. I didn't know mom still had this!* Savy used the metal locks on the side to open it and couldn't believe they still worked. She saw letters from her mom. A dried corsage was lying in the suitcase with a little note.

To my Savy,

Never forget how a man should treat you. I love you to the moon and back!

Love, Dad

Savy remembered, *every year, my dad would take me to a dance to ensure I knew how to be treated. When I got too big to go to the dance, we started going out to eat, to a movie, or anything I wanted to do. He would pull my chair out and open doors. I always felt like a princess. Like I mattered. Boy, did I know how to choose them*! She thought to herself.

She found an old ring in a small pocket of the suitcase and put it on her finger. Mom always kept everything. *It was an old promise ring from my first serious boyfriend,* she remembered. They had dated for about two years. *When we broke up, I tried to trash the ring. Mom must've grabbed it out of the trash. Little did I know I'd be running across it someday. I picked up some other things; a piece of old rope, a necklace I don't remember seeing, and my old class ring. I picked up a wooden cross my mom had brought me back from Israel. After my dad became saved at a tent revival, he was so on fire for the Lord he had to go and see the Promise Land. They had to save a lot of money to go on that trip. My mom always said, "I wanna go before I'm raptured!"*

So, my dad worked a lot of overtime. They had a jar with a cactus on it, and they called it their "Dream Jar." I remember when they came home. They gave me a cross made out of olive wood. Their eyes lit up, telling me about going to Jesus's tomb, visiting the Wailing Wall, floating in the Dead Sea, and they were rebaptized in the Jordan River. I asked why they wanted to be baptized again...weren't they already saved? Their response to me was, "Who wouldn't want to be baptized where Jesus Himself was baptized?" With my parents, it wasn't a matter of their salvation. They just wanted to experience every bit of Jesus they could.

I didn't understand why they wanted to go to this desert of a place instead of saving their money for Hawaii or Barbados. Put me on a beach, and I'm good all day long. For me, that was a calming spot. When they got back home, they were glad to be back in Tennessee, but they told me the moment they stepped off the plane in Israel, they immediately felt this sense of home.

Strange, I thought. *How could a place like that feel like home?* I held the wooden cross to my heart and picked up my old Bible from when I was a little girl. I began to thumb through the pages and remembered the picture where a whale swallowed Jonah. It was my favorite story.

I couldn't imagine being swallowed by a whale! Savy thought. Jonah wouldn't go to Nineveh, where God had told him to go, and part of his punishment was being swallowed by the giant whale. *I often wondered if this actually happened, but I never believed my family would disappear either. I guess you can't say it would never happen now.*

I reached in and pulled out my brother's old hat with a fishhook on the side of the bill. It was worn and frayed. I flipped it over and there was a verse written, Mark 1:17 (NKJV) "Follow me, and I will make you fishers of men." *I really didn't get it,* I thought, *even now.*

So many times, my mom would try to explain the things happening in the world. I remember this drive I took with my mom. It was nighttime, and the windows were down. I could hear the crickets outside as we drove down those old country roads. She shared with me her struggle when she was young. She explained that for a long time, she felt like she was in it alone. She would walk to church by herself, but every night her dad would start drinking and wouldn't stop. He was hard to get along with, and most times, she just kept out of his way. Sometimes she would just sit in her room and try to listen to music, trying to cover up the noise and her thoughts.

When she went to church, she felt that everything was okay. At that moment, God had her in a calmer place. She told me all this because she wanted me to stop running. "You know the truth, Savy, and you just keep running." "Mom, I'm not running. I'm just busy. I don't have extra time to be involved in a church. I don't have time to study. I have my work I have to continue to focus on. On my off days, I feel like I'm still working. I can't leave work at work like other people. I'm constantly rewriting papers and researching laws." On that drive, my mom had a tear stream down her face.

"I worry about you, Savy." I grabbed mom's hand, "Momma, you don't have to worry about me. I'm okay." "Oh, Savy, you just think you're okay." "The Lord gives us evidence that He is real, and He will come back. We will meet Him in the clouds and be taken." "Taken? Vanished?" Savy said, not really believing that one day this would in fact happen. *The rapture of the church theology seems like a stretch,* Savy thought. Her mom continued, "Savy, it is real. In 1 Thessalonians 4 it explains how the dead in Christ will rise first, and then we who are alive and remain shall be caught up together with them in the clouds to meet the Lord in the air. That means exactly what it says. The Bible is infallible. Savy, it will happen. We don't know when, and I just want all my loved ones to believe. I don't want anyone to miss His coming and being snatched up." I was silent. I didn't know what to think. "When a child steps into oncoming traffic, the parents do something. They grab that child and protect them. He is protecting us from His wrath. When we are true believers in Christ we will be taken from this earth before God allows His wrath to ensue upon the whole earth."

For some reason, emotions, truth, and catching up always came out in car rides. We were very close, but that was until I chose a career path over my family. I mean, I came home on the holidays...okay, most holidays. I guess the longer I stayed gone, the easier it was. If I didn't come home, I didn't have to say goodbye or try and plan another date for the next time I would be in town.

I glanced down at my favorite story,

> Jonah 2:2-5,7 (NKJV) "I cried out to the Lord because of my affliction, And He answered me. Out of the belly of Sheol I cried, *And* You heard my voice. For You cast me into the deep, Into the heart of the seas, and the floods surrounded me; All Your billows and Your waves passed over me. Then I said 'I have been cast out of Your sight; Yet I will look again toward Your holy temple.' The waters surrounded me, *even* to my soul; the deep closed around me; Weeds were wrapped around my head. When my soul fainted within me, I remembered the Lord; And my prayer went up to You, into Your holy temple."

Sitting in that dark hole under the stairs watching the cast of the light wave from above my head, I imagined being in the belly of that whale. I ran, I thought. *I ran like Jonah, not wanting to go to Nineveh. Why did I not listen? Why did Jonah not listen? Now I'm stuck here in the belly just like Jonah? Can I not have more chances? I closed my eyes and could feel the heaviness of not listening sooner. My soul felt surrounded by the deep waters of the sea. I imagined myself in the darkness of the deep waters and I felt the seaweed wrapping around my neck and up around my head. Darkness and loneliness were all I felt at that moment. I couldn't breathe. Breathe! I kept telling myself! Just breathe!* Significant anxiety rushed over my whole body, and I felt like I was going to faint. I pushed open the door, climbed out from under the stairs, and collapsed on the cold hardwood floor. My legs were still halfway in the doorway. Closing my eyes, I broke out into a cold sweat.

Tucker walked up the front porch steps. He had just finished taking care of the chickens and was about to knock on the door. He heard a clunk and he hurriedly reached for the doorknob and opened the door. He was alarmed to see me lying there unconscious! He rushed to my side to take my pulse. I started to come to, seeing the faint lines of Tucker's head. My pulse was weak and thready. He grabbed a rag off the kitchen counter and soaked it in cold water. I began to wake up and feel a little clearer. After wringing out the rag, Tucker placed the rag on my head.

"Tucker, I'm so embarrassed. I don't know...maybe I got too hot?" Tucker looked at me gently. "Savy," he began, "You don't have to explain anything to me. I'm just glad I came when I did!" "I found letters that mom had written, and I sat under there a while looking at everything." "Under the stairs? For how long?" Tucker said, with his forehead wrinkled. "Yes, mom told me the letters were under the stairs. I...I'm not sure how long." "Well, let me grab them for you, so you don't have to go back under there. I imagine it is hot under there." "You really don't have to do...," I began. Before I could finish, Tucker crawled under the stairs and gathered everything up.

"Savy?" "Yes," I replied, wiping my head with the wet rag. "You want the blue suitcase and this small Bible that's lying on the floor?" "Yes. I must've dropped it when I passed out. Do you see anything else?" "There's a key on a nail in here." "I guess we should leave it. I have no clue what that is to." Tucker came out with a little smirk on his face. "What is it?" Savy asked. "I just think this is cute," holding up her little, small black Bible. I smiled back. "That was mine when I was a wee lass," I joked. "If only I would've listened to what my parents kept trying to tell me." "Well, I guess that goes for the both of us then." I looked up at Tucker. "You should've listened to your parents too?" "No," Tucker replied. "I should've listened to yours."

There was silence. As I was getting up from the floor, Tucker rushed over to me. "Savy, go slow. Be careful." He helped me get to a chair and moved the overstuffed, plaid ottoman under my feet. I smiled, "Tucker?" He glanced up at me. "I'm really okay." He sat beside me and began talking to me about my dad.

"I noticed your dad was a humble countryman, quiet at times, but when it came to the Bible and talking about Jesus...he was a different man." Tucker chuckled a little, "He could recite verses and pray like nobody I've ever heard. One time I had kidney stones." He laughed again. "I was on the tractor and started to feel the worst pain of my life." Savy smiled, "Was it like they say? Did you birth a baby?" "A small one," Tucker joked. "That man got me in the car and prayed on the way to the hospital." They were both laughing. He continued, "I mean, I was saying, "I'm going to die!" "A little dramatic, don't you think?" I asked. "Maybe...have you ever had a kidney stone?" Tucker replied, smiling. "Well, no, I can't say I have, actually." "Many times, he would ask me if I believed, and if I ever wanted to receive Christ, but as you can tell, well, I'm still here." "So that goes for the both of us, huh?" I said, biting the side of my lip.

"So, what about your family?" I asked. "My mom and sister are gone." "Your dad?" I inquired. "Well, my dad passed early." "I'm sorry," I replied. "Well, it was a long time ago. I still miss him very much." "We were close growing up, and one day his heart...just stopped working. We were picking tomatoes out of the garden one day. I thought maybe he was getting too hot. He just started breathing hard and had to lay down." I could tell that it still bothered Tucker. "How old were you?" "I was about fifteen." "Goodness Tucker, that's terrible." *I noticed the line that seemed to define Tucker's arms.* I had to quickly look away. "Is there anything you need before I leave? I should probably be going," Tucker said. "Yes," I replied. "Yes, you need something?" "No! I mean...yes." I was frazzled. "Yes, I should be going?" Tucker said confused. "No! I didn't mean that either." I frowned. "Thank you for coming and helping me, but Tucker there is something," Savy said with a curious look. "Anything," Tucker replied. "Can you walk down the steps with me and help me figure out what the key goes to?" "Sure," Tucker responded. "I was curious myself, but I didn't know if you felt up to it." "I'm feeling a little better, and I know I won't be able to sleep tonight if I don't figure out what that key is for."

They went under the stairs. Savy lifted the key off the nail and Tucker turned on the light. "I am not seeing anything in here," Tucker said looking for clues. "Why would they have this in here if there wasn't a door?" Savy said. "Maybe there is something in another area?" They walked upstairs and covered every square inch inside the house. Tucker began pounding areas of the walls as if he was looking for a stud or hollow area in different rooms to find something. "Okay maybe we are just crazy. Maybe this goes to the barn?" Savy questioned to Tucker.

They started toward the barn. They searched the stalls and then went into the tack room where the supplies were stored. Tucker began feeling the floorboards in the tack room. They glanced at each other in wonder when one end of a floorboard came up. "Whaaat?" Savy said in unbelief.

Tucker pulled it up and they saw an industrial looking ladder leading into a dark hole. "Are you going down there?" Savy said looking at Tucker. "I thought we were doing this together," he replied with a smile. "Okay," Savy said breathing in a big sigh. "But I need you to go first." "You need me?" Tucker questioned. Savy flushed red and felt a little embarrassed. Tucker just chuckled a bit and began descending into the darkness. Savy grabbed a flashlight from the tack room shelf and held it over Tucker's head. The light was a bit dim, but she was surprised it worked at all.

The underground tunnel became wider, and boxes of supplies were piled up everywhere. "We are going to have to come back later," Savy said to Tucker. "The flashlight is about dead. I don't want to have to feel my way back. This is creepy." Tucker replied, "Okay, we will come back later and try to go through this stuff."

For the first time in my life, I didn't know how to respond to these goose bumps and this excited but nervous feeling. I took a deep breath and held my hands over my eyes. Oh goodness, what am I doing? This is not the time to have any sort of romance. Nick was kind of a boyfriend if you even wanted to call him that. He was a starving artist. Literally, starving, and now that I think about it...he was probably more moochin' off the fact that I worked, and he could never come up with the rent. I kept him up more than anything. I would work all day, and when I came home, he would go and play with his band members. We had weekends together more than anything. I enjoyed that after working all week. I didn't have to worry about a full-blown relationship, it was just nice having someone to be with. He was an excellent musician, and I always wondered if he would make it big in the music industry. So, for the most part, I allowed myself to be a part of his dream.

Tucker, on the other hand, was completely different. Maybe it was because I had just passed out and was feeling shaky, but I could feel my knees buckle. He seemed to be a hardworking man to keep up my daddy's farm. Daddy's gone, he isn't getting paid, but he continues to keep the farm running. Doing this shows his heart for my family and his dedication to his work. I vaguely remember Daddy talking about Tucker a few times, and from what I can remember, my family was pretty fond of his eagerness to work. If I could erase time and ask more questions, that would be good, but if daddy ever got the clue that I was asking about him, that might be awkward.

I've got too much to worry about! Why is my mind so focused on him! He seems caring and humble. I wonder if he genuinely was humble or if he knew how good-looking he really was? Come on, Savy! I thought. *I cannot get into any kind of relationship. Besides, I should've listened to my parents. I wouldn't even be in this situation had I listened. Even Tucker had said the same thing that rang in my head over and over, "I should've listened too."*

"That has to lead somewhere." We walked back to the house and were standing on the porch. "I know you are tired," Tucker said, putting his hand on my shoulder. "Do you think you will be able to rest?" he said, as he looked into my eyes. I loved the way his eyes crinkled when he smiled. "As best as I can. I guess," I said, as I opened the door. "Tucker!" He turned as he was walking back to his truck. "Thank you," I said. *I pushed my back against the door as I closed it and, put my hand to my forehead.* Half to myself, and half out loud I said, *"Okay, Lord, I don't know what I'm doing."*

Savy went to bed tossing and turning with two things on her mind.

1. Tucker
2. What did that key go to?

Chapter 5

The afternoon sun was letting the animals know it was feed time. Henry had just gone and gotten feed from the store. While he was in the store, it didn't seem anyone was running the store. He looked around, and not a soul was to be found. So, he decided to check the back for feed. As he went to the back, he saw a younger gentleman. "Sir?" he looked up at Henry. "I just need feed for my farm." "Go on back and get what you need." "I can pay you," Henry replied. "No, just get what you need to keep your farm going. I don't know how I'll ever be able to keep my father's store running." "Well, I'll just get a few bags. I can't afford more than that right now." "Just pay me for those bags, and I'll give you more than you need." Henry didn't know what to think. *This nice young man was just giving me feed for free?* "Just back your truck up, and I'll help you load it."

Henry went and backed his truck up, and started to load feed with him. He just kept loading feed into Henry's truck. "I...I don't know what to say. Thank you." Henry was a little surprised by the man's generosity. "Is your family gone?" "Everything is gone," the young man replied. "Right now, I feel like I'm in this weird sci-fi movie. I thought I would never see a day like this. I went to college and came home when all this happened." Henry just listened. "I partied way too hard. Didn't care about anything but drinking and girls. My parents stopped paying for school, which woke me up a little, I guess, but not enough. Now I'm here not having a clue what to do." "Do you know why your parents are gone?" Henry asked. The kid kind of smiled a bit. "Are you about to tell me because of some fairy tale of our Creator taking them home?" "God took them home." "How can you even be so sure of that?"

The young man looked down at his boots. Henry just stared at him, knowing he had felt this way and had the same questions. "Look, everythin' my Maggie told me has either happened or started to happen. When she left me, I started readin' in her Bible because she tried her hardest to get me to commit my life to Christ. Her Bible has all these notes and messages. I can't explain everythin' to you yet, but it makes more sense than anythin' they are sayin' on the news right now. All I can tell you is you have to get ready to stand strong." Henry's eyes filled up with tears. "Here's my address. If you ever need to talk, just come on by. You're always welcome." Henry shut the tailgate and got into his truck. He rolled down his window. "I mean that now. We are all lost just tryin' to find our way in this evil dyin' world." The young man nodded his head, thinking about Henry's words, as Henry said, "Thank you for helpin' me."

When Henry was feeding the cows, he noticed one of his heifers was gone. He rode his four-wheeler all over the farm, trying to find his lost cow. When he finally discovered her lying dead in the woods, outside the pasture, she had been butchered, cut open like someone had just taken the meat and left her there for the crows. Henry was so upset and had to call someone to come and get her. He just couldn't believe the world was getting so dark. This wasn't the first time someone had been on his property. Just a day or so ago, he went to feed the chickens; someone had opened the cage and stolen some of his birds. People were looting too much, and he didn't know how long all this could go on. His stomach felt uneasy thinking about what would come of his farm.

Darkness fell as Henry was finishing up feeding and noticed someone coming up the driveway. He felt to make sure he had his gun on him. This young woman got out of the car. She was in her pajamas. Henry realized it was Virginia. The last time he'd seen her, she was pregnant. She lived just a little piece down the road. "When did you have the baby?" She replied, "Two days ago, but my milk hasn't come in yet and I can't afford formula." She blushed feeling embarrassed talking about this with Henry, but she knew she had to do something. "Just a sec," Henry said as he went into the house and brought her a case full of milk. "Fresh milk for you there, darlin'."

Virginia, grateful for the kind gesture, hugged Henry, and tears welled up in her eyes. "I can hardly deal with all this, Henry. If I'd just committed my life to Christ. I had Livy right after the chaos began." She leaned against the car as Henry was putting the milk crate in the back seat. Wiping her tears, she continued, "I had gone to the hospital the night before the 'Big Change' happened. My contractions were getting closer and closer together. All of a sudden nurses were screaming. Running down the hall. I tried to get up and go see what was happening. Someone shut the door on me. That's when I hit the nurse button and looked out the window of my room. I had never seen anything like it. I quickly turned on the news and saw the many disappearances." Henry looked into Virginia's eyes. She looked scared. "After I had Livy I demanded they discharge me. I told them I had to go home. Bret was with me during all of that, but he was freaking out not knowing what to do."

"You know I'm here for ya. We are in a mess for sure now, aren't we? Hey, listen, Virginia. We are goin' to be smart, and if worst comes to worst, well, we will do what we have to do. Now don't fret. Is your boyfriend still with you?" "Yes," she responded, as she sniffled back the tears. "Well, good, tell him to make a trip and come get a gun. I'm goin' give him a lesson." "Okay. Okay," Virginia repeated. She wiped her tears, thanked Henry, and kissed him on the cheek. Her father had been good friends with Henry. She knew she could come to him. "Thank you." As she held her hand out the window, Henry grabbed her hand. "Hey, you're goin' to be okay girl. We've got each other. I'm learnin' a lot readin' Mag's old Bible." He let go of her hand and watched her drive down the long driveway. He softly whispered, "Lord, please help her and that sweet baby."

After coming in and eating supper, Henry sat in front of the television. He watched as the world was turned upside down. There was devastation. People were in panic mode. They were going into stores, stealing, and gunning others down. Henry had made it a point not to go back to town after the showdown at the gas station. The talking heads were discussing microchipping because things were getting out of hand. They needed to track people, to be able to have access and to know where people were. They explained how things would be a lot safer and more secure. A man they continued congratulating on the technology was in the public eye. They began to talk about how he had more of the answers to get us through all of the chaos. They made sure to bark his praise repeatedly. "It's startin'," Henry said to himself, switching off the television and getting ready for bed.

Chapter 6

Savy woke up, and immediately opened another letter from her mother after making coffee.

My Dear Sweet Savy,

I know you must have a lot of questions. So, let me start with there will be 3 ½ years when people will continue looking for a savior. The Jewish people in Israel are looking for this savior, and they will be deceived. They are looking for someone who's going to get them through these rough years. Then after the first 3 ½ years, the Antichrist will rise to power in the temple made by the Jewish people. He will make everyone have a mark on their forehead or on their right hand to be able to buy and sell. This will sound like a really safe and secure thing to do. After all, no one can steal your information, and if someone kills you, this technology will be able to shut off due to a dropping body temperature. Anything that you buy will be only through this chip. If someone pays you money, it will be through this chip. Therefore, you will automatically be taxed. This is a cashless society, which will answer what everyone has been looking for. This Antichrist that comes to power is very real. The Antichrist will also have the false prophet working in his favor.

I'm sure you've met Tucker by now. Please give him the letter with his name on it. Tucker is a good man. He works hard, and your dad thinks a lot of him. If you need anything, please let Tucker know. Your dad and I trust Tucker. Don't open his letter, just give it to him. Savy, I know you're curious as always but just continue to trust. There is not a lot left to trust. You see, Savy, God was restraining the Lawless One, the Antichrist. He was restraining him from coming to power by His Holy Spirit. When your dad and I accepted Christ into our hearts, His spirit filled us, and we tried as best we could to live for Him daily. Although, if you're left reading this, I feel I have failed Him. I know what you're thinking, Savy, but as a momma, you always want the best for your kids.

Now, this is your burden, Savy girl. You have to be as wise as a serpent and harmless as a dove. Matthew 10:16. It's time to put on the full armor of God. Ephesians 6:10-20. Savy, gird your waist with truth, put on the breastplate of righteousness, your feet with the preparation of the Gospel of Peace, taking the shield of faith. With that shield, you will be able to protect yourself from the fiery darts of the wicked one. Put on the helmet of salvation and the sword of the Spirit, which is The Word of God.

These times that you are walking in are so uncertain. If you hold to Him, He will reward you, and you will have eternal salvation and peace. However, if you don't and fold to Satan, your eternity will be spent in Hell. Savy, this is serious, and I pray as I'm in Heaven that you are serious. The things I read about before leaving this earth were like Sodom. I stayed up nights on end, praying for our country, world, leaders, and most of all, YOU. There is nothing that those talking heads on television are going to tell you that you don't already know. DISCONNECT. They are held to a standard of the world. If you have accepted Christ, you are no longer of this world.

Now I don't know where you're going to go from here, but wherever you go, make sure you are smart. Please don't let Tucker get too far, Savy. He's a good one. Your dad believes he would risk his life for anyone. He can shoot a gun. He can fish and grow crops. He can live off the land. I'm just worried about you. I'm afraid as I'm writing this letter, that I hope you never have to read.

May God Protect You.

Love,

Mom

Oh wow, I thought to myself, *that's heavy*. I looked down at my cell phone. It was 8:00am. I pulled the blinds to see if Tucker was still feeding. His truck was parked in the driveway. Still not totally dressed, I threw on my robe and pulled on my mom's muck boots. "Hey, Tucker," I yelled out. He waved and walked toward me. I was holding the letter in my hand, still unsure about giving him such a thing, but it did seem that my parents knew him pretty well. "Hey, good morning," he said, smiling.

"Morning to you. Look, I know I look terrible, but I was just reading..." "Some of those letters from under the stairs?" "Yes...well, and momma wanted me to give this one to you." As I handed it to him, he looked a bit surprised. "Yes, I know, crazy...right? Well, I don't know what it said. I didn't read it or anything...I mean, I didn't think I should...after all-" "No! Savy. Savy, it's fine. Thank you," Tucker said, cutting me off and ensuring I knew he was okay with it. "I will leave you to it." I went back inside with the screen door shutting behind me.

I got one glimpse of myself in the mirror and couldn't believe I just went out there looking like this! I mean, after all, I've never been a girl that looks good naturally! My hair looked a mess, and my face discolored a bit without makeup. I hopped in the shower quickly; letting the water hit my face. I thought about Tucker and his smile. *I wondered what it would be like to kiss him. I felt my face turn red at the thought of kissing him.* My body began to feel a little weak. *What in the world was*

I thinking? Why didn't my parents ever introduce me to him before this mess? Although, I didn't come home enough to remember if I had seen him. His hands looked strong...I don't know where these thoughts kept coming from...

Tucker sat down on the porch steps while opening the letter labeled *Tucker* on the front of the envelope.

Dear Tucker,

If you're reading this, we were raptured and taken to Heaven, and you were left. There are a lot of things that are going to happen that you need to be ready for. I honestly had hoped that you would never have to read this and endure the things that are about to happen in the next seven years. If you're reading this, then my daughter Savy gave you the letter. I have prayed a lot over the last couple of years for you and my daughter. Several times I tried to get her to come home for you two to have a chance to meet.

My prayer has been that you wouldn't have to be here for what is to come during the Great Tribulation. I have prayed for years that both you and Savy would turn your hearts to Christ and that you would allow Him to lead you. Well, here you are reading this letter. I honestly could never imagine the day that this would all take place. Tucker, there are going to be extremely hard times. We were not taken by aliens, killed by a virus, or kidnapped. God took us. I know that many people don't have an explanation, but I'm telling you, we have been caught up in the clouds to meet our Lord and Savior. It may sound a bit of a fairy tale to you, but it's not.

Some things are going to take place, and I need you to be there and watch over my Savy for me. If there is anything at all that her dad would ask of you, it would be this. He sings your praises all the time about how hard of a worker you are. He thought a lot about you. He tells me you could keep yourselves alive if you had to. He says you can hunt, fish, live off the land, and fix just about anything. So, get ready because that's how hard times will get for y'all.

I need you to watch over my Savy. She is strong herself, and I don't doubt she will teach you some things. Two is better than one, and I need y'all to take these words seriously. I've explained a lot to Savy, but there will be a man with all the answers that will rise to power. He is the Antichrist. He will try and be God. He will try and proclaim it. Do not receive the mark of the beast. This mark may seem like a more comfortable lifestyle, but Tucker just get used to life not being easy. If there ever was an Armageddon, you're about to see the worst war ever after all of this is over.

I want you and Savy to read Revelation 13:11-18, which explains the mark I'm talking about. Please don't let her out of your sight. I mean, who else do y'all have right now but each other? Scott showed you where his guns and ammo are. I suggest you get them, use them, and teach Savy how to shoot. I trust you to use your best judgement for protection. Remember, this is not a battle against flesh and blood. It is a battle against darkness.

This is a time to get serious, like I've always tried telling Savy. Being a Christian is serious business. In my Bible is the Roman Road to Salvation. These scriptures will give you some understanding of what it means to be a Christian. As the two of you think and discuss these things, if you decide to become Christians, I've written Savy out a sinner's prayer. I know you must decide these things on your own, but how much more proof does anyone need? You must endure these things until the very end and pray that the Lord cuts these days short for you during this time.

There will be signs that begin to happen on earth; great earthquakes, rivers turning into blood, the stars will fall, Christians will be hunted, brought to authorities, and killed, and great famines will take place on the earth. So much the news and scientists will try to explain away, but just know that God is letting His wrath come down for a time. He is allowing Satan to take control for but a time. He is allowing the lawlessness because the people left never heard his still small voice. Maybe they chose to ignore like you and Savy did. Perhaps they thought they had enough time when they really didn't.

Just know that time is up, and now you will have to be willing to die for Christ. To die for Christ is to live eternal. This is a time to be strong. Not only strong on the outside but just as much on the inside. Tucker, if it seems I'm coming on strong in this letter, there is no time to waste. My two kids are the most extraordinary things God has given me, but Savy just couldn't accept Him for some reason. I'm sure I'm praying for y'all right now in Heaven. Even the saints cry out, asking how much longer, Lord! Revelation 6:10.

Hold Strong, Tucker.

Love,

Carma

P.S. Isn't she beautiful? Watch how her eyes sparkle and her dimples light up when she smiles.

Well, thought Tucker, *that didn't come on strong at all.* He kind of smiled at her mention about Savy. He actually had noticed her dimples and her smile. She was beautiful, but how could he take on this role when they had just met. It did bother him what all he didn't know. What would they have to go through together during this time? He remembered Scott telling him bits and pieces, but it was way over his head. What bothered him most was now having to experience this because he didn't act when he knew he should've. He felt God tugging at him too, but just couldn't accept. He felt as if he didn't understand it all, or it didn't even make sense. *I mean, it seemed that things needed some scientific proof. How to know there is a God or not. Now I'm too late, and the evidence has been whisked away. I thought more proof was coming, apparently. The proof I wish I weren't a part of. If I'd only accepted and listened to Scott when I felt the Lord tug at my heart.*

After getting out of the shower, she threw on her holey blue jeans and a flannel shirt. She put on a little bit of face and stepped onto the porch. "Hey Tucker, you wanna come in? You don't have to sit out here. I'm sorry, I just knew I needed to freshen up." "No, it's okay. I'm going to head home now that the chores are finished." "Are you sure? I'll make breakfast?" "Tonight?" "You want breakfast tonight?" grinned Savy. "Sure!" Tucker said. "After I feed, we will plan on supper. Your mom...she was a good woman. I sure miss your dad too." "Was the letter okay?" Savy asked. "I'm sure it was pretty deep. There's a lot I still don't know or even understand." "Yeah," he replied. "Yes, it was good. Things I needed to be reminded of and to watch for." "Savy," he grabbed for her hand. "We are going to make it through. There is no other option." Savy's eyes filled with tears. He let her hand go as she wiped her eyes. "Thanks for that, Tucker, and you're right. There is no other option. Tucker, would you actually drive me to Jules? She should be at her sister's." "Yes, I don't mind at all. I can drop you off with her. Do you want me to wait for you?" Tucker asked. "No, I will have Jules drive me back." She smiled and grabbed her purse ready to head out.

Tucker pulled up to Jules' sister's house and Savy jumped out of the car. She ran up the steps, opened the creaky screen door, and knocked on the front door. Jules' sister lived on their grand-father's property. They were close and her sister took care of him. Jules opened the door and immediately wrapped her arms around Savy. "Oh, girl I've missed you!" She glanced outside and noticed Tucker. Placing her hands on Savy's shoulders she felt excitement for Savy. Looking her in the eyes with a smirk. "Honey! What in the world? He is FINE!" she exclaimed. "Okay, explain yourself please." "Okay, will you drive me home? I just wanted to check on y'all. I will explain everything then." "No girl, you will explain now," Savy waved bye to Tucker. "Thank you!" she yelled. She watched as he pulled out of the driveway.

Jules poured a glass of sweet tea and they sat and talked about everything. They talked about Tucker, the Bible, how Jules will take care of her grandfather now that she and her grandfather are the only ones left in her family, and about the supplies found and the secret tunnel under the tack room. "What were your parents thinking? I mean to prepare like that? That is totally God, Savy." "Yes, it is. I honestly think they were just listening to God's push to be like Joseph. That a famine was coming, and they needed to prepare." Jules sat there in awe of the news. "Jules," Savy said reaching for her hand. "We are in this together. My place is definitely yours. Hear me when I say that." "Of course. I just have to play everything out. I have to be here right now, but I know where to go." "Promise me Jules," Savy said firmly. "I promise. Now, Savy, continue on about Tucker!" "So, he is coming for breakfast tonight." "Is it a date?" "I don't even know, but he is seriously giving me these...I want to know you better vibes," Savy said kind of nervous and giddy. "Girl!" "I know! I know," repeated Savy. "It's like he wants to be there for me. I feel embarrassed at times though. I've had some rough episodes with my heart." "Like are you trying to pass out more?" Jules said, concerned. "Yes, but I'll just have to try and keep my salt intake up; to ensure I have electrolytes." Jules worried about Savy ever since high school, when the episodes began to come on more frequently.

Chapter 7

She held the cross on her necklace between her fingers as she slid the cross from side to side. She was thinking about her conversation with Henry. She found the Bible her Jenny and the grandkids had given her. It's funny, her Jenny became a mother later in life, just like she had. Partly because of her career as a dancer, and partly just fate. She held her leather Bible that had golden letters on the bottom right-hand corner which said Manna. It always made her smile that they said Manna instead of Nana. Jenny had a girl and two boys. People seemed really mixed up with genders these days, but those three were true genders to the core. Those boys loved to get muddy, catch frogs, and skip rocks across the pond. They would live outside if their mother would let them.

Sweet little Mae was always doing her makeup and dressing in her mama's heels. She was a priss pot (a true dainty girl who loved girly attire) for sure! She missed them so much that she felt like her body ached inside. When Jenny brought them home from the hospital, everyone was so excited! Jenny didn't want anyone telling her how to be a mom, so most of the time, Lou would stand back and just let her figure it out until she couldn't. Then she would call her momma crying. "I can't get her to stop crying, momma. She won't let us sleep, and I'm so tired, momma. Steve has to work tomorrow, and my head is killing me." "I'll be over in about 15 minutes." Manna saved the day as always. "What would I do without you, mom?" Jenny would say. "You would do just fine," Manna would reply. Lou's grandchildren grew to call her Manna. They loved her so much and she loved them. Anytime Jenny needed her she was there.

As Lou thought about her conversation with Henry, she began to feel a change in her heart. She held her Bible in her hands and looked at the golden worn pages. Lou opened it and noticed the verses on manna. Her daughter had highlighted scripture for Lou before gifting it to her. Exodus 16:31 (NKJV) said: And the house of Israel called its name Manna. And it *was* like white coriander seed, and the taste of it *was* like wafers *made* with honey.

Along with sweet handwriting on the front saying, Manna, you're sweet like honey. Lou thought to herself, *when I turned to Revelation, it seems much like the end, as Sis said. I saw scrolls, seals, trumpets, the two witnesses, and beasts. I can't even wrap my brain around what all this means.* Lou sighed, feeling overwhelmed, and just bowed my head and prayed.

"Lord, obviously, this is something, and I totally missed the boat. I'm so sorry I didn't listen. You had blessed me so much, and I see that it's my fault that I didn't even respond to you. That I didn't accept. I don't have a clue what the end of this Bible means. I don't understand it, Lord. I pray that you help my unbelief. Help me to turn to you. Help me understand what some of this means and what this is all about. All I know right now is I want to see my family again. You have everything I love. You gave me that, and I took it for granted. I'm sorry, Lord, and I hope it's not too late for me to become saved." Ms. Lou sat the Bible down on the coffee table.

She reached for the phone and started to dial her great nephew, Andy. He was her sister's grandson and she called him her nephew because they were so close. "Andy, hey, it's Manna Lou. Give me a call when you get this message. I need to talk to you. Love you." She hung the phone up after no answer. He would call back. He always did. Andy worked as a veterinarian. He specialized in small animals. Everyone thinks a lot about their pets nowadays. They even get their teeth cleaned for three hundred dollars! *I would like to see the owner's mouth to see if their teeth were that clean. I have never heard of dental bills for your pets! Outrageous*, thought Lou. Andy stayed pretty busy, but he loved his job. Right now, business was still pretty good. He called just the other day and shared that they had a lot of strays they had been trying to find homes for since the "Big Change." Apparently, that's what people were calling it. So, he has been busier with that than anything else.

Lou walked outside to sit on the porch and smoke a cigarette. It was raining, and she could hear the trickle as the rain came out of the gutters. Rain always made her feel at peace, and for the first time since the "Big Change," she took a deep breath. She exhaled the smoke and thought again about her conversation with Henry. She didn't know what to do about his offer, but she did feel lonely and sometimes scared, now that her kids and grandkids were gone. They had come over almost daily. They were her whole world.

Should she learn to shoot a gun? Would she actually pull the trigger if she had to? Henry seemed like a really nice man. She didn't know what she would have done if it hadn't been for Savy and Henry that day. They risked their own lives that day. Amid all the chaos, they could've just worried about themselves, but they couldn't leave me for some reason. That meant something.

She closed her eyes, and felt the inhale of nicotine in her lungs and slowly exhaled and flicked her ashes from her cigarette onto the ground. She looked at the puddles of water in the yard and watched as the rain fell from the sky and made wrinkles in the water. A tear rolled down her cheek as she could imagine her sweet grandbabies with their rain boots splashing in the puddle. She sniffled and put the bud out. The sun was going down, and she went inside and locked her door.

As she took her coat off, the phone started to ring. She hurried over to the phone. "Hello?" "Hello, this is the last time to renew your car's extended warran-." Lou slammed down the phone! It's amazing they are still calling after all this. Yes, why yes! I need to extend my car's warranty! *Oh goodness, let's do this,* thought Lou. They ticked her off. They called no matter how many times she told them off! They just kept calling back.

The phone rang again. "I don't need your-..." "Ms. Lou, it's Savy. I made it to Tennessee and wanted to call and check on you. Henry told me he came by." "Oh yes, that Henry is so sweet. He has a big heart," answered Lou. "Well, we've been keeping in touch, and I wanted you to know we are both here for you. I've thought a lot about you being there by yourself all alone, and it bothers me."

Lou grabbed her cross around her neck and thought about everything again. She did get scared by herself at night. "Well, thank y'all for being so generous. I don't really know what to think about Henry's offer, but I will definitely think about it. How was your trip to Tennessee?" "I'm still here trying to sort through everything, but I really thought about coming and making sure you're okay." "I'm fine, Savy. Don't worry your little head about me. My grandnephew Andy is here if I need him."

"Alright, well, just wanted to call and see how you were. I'll talk to you later."
"Alright, bye-bye."

She laid in bed that night with a light from the bathroom on. She always had to have a little light, so she didn't fall as she got up. She tossed and turned, thinking about the break-in that just happened down the road. People were getting braver and braver. Looting and crimes were up, and people were getting desperate. The more she thought about Henry's offer, the more she thought about how that might be what she needed to do. However, she may need to call Savy back in the morning and see what her plans were. It was a good idea to be safe and have people around. If Savy was coming back, maybe she would want to move in with her, or perhaps that was just hopeful thinking.

She picked up her book of poetry she read at night. It helped lift her spirits even if they did seem to be living in this dark world now. It appeared all the light had gone out of the world. As she was reading, she heard the doorknob on her front door.

She could hear steps on her porch and someone talking outside. Ms. Lou got up and out of bed and closed and locked her bedroom door. She went to get the gun out of the safe. Henry was right. He needed to teach her how to use a gun. She thought if anything, the gun would scare them away. So, she grabbed the phone. "Andy, someone is messing with my front door."

"Stay on the phone with me, Manna Lou. I'm sending the police to come to check it out, and I'm on my way." She felt so nervous inside. "Okay," she whispered. She prayed silently that they would just go away. She couldn't hear anything else. "Maybe they went to another house," she whispered. "I don't hear them anymore." "Stay on the phone with me and don't hang up. Someone should be there soon." "I think they may be gone." She looked through her bedroom window blinds to see if she could see anything. She saw a flash of light headed in the other direction.

Maybe they were going to find a more accessible house to break into. She had a deadbolt on her front door. "I think they are leaving," she repeated. "Just stay in your bedroom." She heard a police car sound its horn once and made her way to the door as Andy stayed on the phone with her. With rollers in her hair and a robe wrapped around her, she opened the door to talk to the officer. "I'm on the phone with my nephew, Andy. He is asking if you will wait with me until he gets here?" "Sure thing ma'am," he replied. "Well, Manna Lou, I'm staying on the phone with you." "Okay."

Andy finally arrived and could tell she was upset and a bit frazzled. The officer explained that they had been covered up with break-ins every night. He told them where Lou lived was more of a retirement neighborhood. People were taking advantage of the older folks living in her neighborhood. The officer told them never hesitate to call, and Andy and Lou thanked him. He let Lou know he would be patrolling her road throughout the night and that he would write up the report in front of her house.

"Manna Lou are you okay?" "Hey, honey! I'm okay, but that did scare me." "I know it did," said Andy. "Andy, I tried calling you earlier today to tell you about my friend Henry. He stopped by the other day, and he's a farmer and has his own place. He asked if I needed a place to stay so I wouldn't get too lonely. What do you think of that?" "Well, Manna Lou, he's the one that helped you and the girl Savy at the gas station, right?" "Yes, he is a very nice man, and sometimes I get a little scared, and I know you're so busy with work. I can't imagine being a burden on you."

"Manna Lou, you're no burden on me, but I live smack dab in the middle of the city, and my apartment building is up three flights of stairs. That's more of my concern. I can help you if you decide to move in, and that was so nice of him to offer." "Maybe we should go and visit him in the morning? I can come often to check up on you if that is what you decide." "Well, honestly, I know it sounds peculiar, but I get a little scared at night. I know there have been some break-ins around me, and now this! I can't imagine leaving all my things..."

"Let's go talk to Henry in the morning then." "Well, okay then. Thanks for being here for me." "We are family Manna Lou." She hugged his neck and fixed him a place on the couch. It took Ms. Lou forever to go to sleep that night. She laid down and felt better now that Andy was there, but she knew he couldn't do this all the time. He could not be this far from the vet's office. She closed her eyes and said a little prayer. "God, thank you for keeping me safe tonight."

Chapter 8

Tucker was so nervous as he was changing into clothes that didn't look like he had been working all day on the farm. He put some dark-washed blue jeans on with a button-up shirt and folded the sleeves up twice. He thought about the letter from Carma the rest of the day. *Savy was pretty. She had dark wavy hair with stark blue eyes. He thought about the feel of her skin when he grabbed her hand. She had smooth skin that felt like silk to his touch. He couldn't believe everything he was experiencing with Savy. These feelings of attraction were different from anything he'd ever had for another woman. He had a girlfriend here or there, but it was just different. He felt something for Savy, even before reading the letter. Although, for some reason, it did make things a little easier knowing how Savy's parents felt.*

Savy was busy getting breakfast ready. She made pancakes, bacon fresh from the hog, and eggs from the hen house. They were just finishing up in the skillet when Tucker knocked on the door. "Hey Tucker." "Would you like me to feed beforehand?" "No, I just took the eggs off the burner. Let's eat, and I'll go out with you after we eat." "Oh, okay! You want to experience some of that farm life, do you?" Tucker said jokingly as he took his boots off. Savy sat her momma's pretty blue willow patterned plates on the table and poured some coffee. "I remember a few things. You know I was raised right here on this farm. How do you like your coffee?"

"Black, please. Is that right, on this farm, huh? Well, maybe you can teach me a thing or two then." "Four-H-er, and don't you forget it!" "Well, if I didn't know any better, I would think our paths probably crossed once or twice." "I remember you from high school, but you were much older than me." "Yes, ma'am, I was. I remember you!" "What?" "Yes, how could I forget. You were a good girl and all about your studies. I see it got you far in life, living in the big city." Savy gave a half-smile. "Maybe I would've been better off here, realizing what all I realize now."

"Savy, look, you cannot change the past, but from the sounds of everything, we must move forward and be prepared." "You're absolutely right, Tucker." "I don't think New York is for me. I feel, for the first time, I can breathe a little. Like I knew I had to come home. Maybe there's something to that." "What's that?" Tucker asked. "Just being able to come home, when everything feels wrong, when it feels like the whole world is falling apart." Savy held her coffee cup with both hands. "I suppose home is where a lot of people want to go back to because that's what they know and where they feel safe. It's their foundation." Tucker picked up the saltshaker on the table. It had a farm pattern on it. Savy could just imagine her mom using it as she cooked. She used to tug on her momma's leg saying, "Let me help momma. Please!" Carma would pick her up and sit her on the counter and teach her how to make biscuits. Coming out of her daydream she said, "it's all so hard." Savy said it knowing there would not be another chance for her to hug her momma's neck. Tucker noticed Savy's teary eyes. She got up, trying to act as if she wasn't going to cry just then. "Okay!" as she rubbed her face. "Show me, Tucker, what you do on this farm. It's really impressive that you have cared so much for my family."

Savy and Tucker put their boots on and walked around the farm together with the flashlight. "Be careful over there. I saw a snake earlier." "What?!!" Tucker laughed as Savy grabbed onto his arm. He looked at her and noticed a small piece of hair had fallen onto her face. His hand swept it out of her face, and his eyes met hers. The moon highlighted the outline of her cheek-bones, and he couldn't believe how beau-tiful she was. She smiled and began to look away, but he touched the side of her face. She looked at him in amazement, feeling like she wanted to kiss him. Her body felt a surge of energy pulsing through her veins. He brought her face closer and moved his body up against hers as he kissed her for the first time. She could feel the strength in his hands as he moved his hands around her waist, pulling her closer. Their lips parted, and Savy took a deep breath. Her head lay on his chest. He had a smell that was a sweet woodsy cologne. He kissed her neck. "Tucker," she whispered. "Yes." "I think we've missed something we could have had a long time ago." "I feel that way too, Savy. I've wanted to kiss you since the first time I saw you," he said softly. "I don't think I can do any of this without you." She had a tear roll down her cheek. Tucker wiped the tear away and touched her chin, making her look up at him. "Hey. You've already got me. It didn't take much at all for me to fall for you." Savy hugged him and just let him hold her.

"Look at those stars, Savy. How did we not believe in a God that big?" "I don't know," she sniffled. "We took it all for granted and listened too much to the world, I guess." He let go of her hand as he dipped the scoop into the feed for the cows. They walked to the chicken coop, and Savy watered the pigs with the hose pipe. When they finished up, they took off their boots and went in. Tucker started a fire in the fireplace. "Would you like a glass of wine?" "Sure," Tucker replied. They sat on the couch watching the fire crackle. Savy let her long wavy hair down from her messy bun and wrapped the hair tie around her wrist along with her other bracelets. She tousled through her hair, getting comfortable and cuddled up to Tucker. "Savy, I like being with you. You make me feel something I have never felt before." He moved his nose against her neck. She could feel shivers go all the way down her spine. She kind of laughed a little and then put her lips up to his scruffy but clean-shaven beard, feeling him move towards her lips. He pressed his lips against hers, starting softly and then firmly against hers. She could feel his hands moving up from her waist. She looked at him, and he could see the dimples in her smile. "Maybe we should slow down a bit," Savy said feeling the rush come over her quickly, trying to deny herself.

He got up from the couch to poke the fire and throw another log on. When he turned back around, he bent down in front of her. She was wrapped in a blanket and noticed the flicker of the fire glistening against his face. He slowly reached for her hand, "Savy, I don't know how we are going to do this at all, but I love you, and I know that I do. Will you marry me?" "What?" Savy questioned. "Will you?" he persisted. "I don't want to have this journey with anyone else. I know this seems all a little fast, but I can see I need you. You have a way of making me feel like I have something. Like a piece of treasure in this dark world. For whatever reason..." He paused as he was thinking of the right thing to say.

"For whatever reason, God has given me this treasure during this time, and now I can't imagine life without you." Savy's tears came back like a flood. "Savy? Are you okay?" She nodded her head, "Yes, I'll marry you," sniffling back tears in a flooded emotion. An emotion of living during this time, an emotion of falling in love with who she knew even her parents loved. "I have fallen so fast for you, but I know this is love. I know this is where I'm supposed to be." She hugged his neck and kissed his cheek. He held onto both of her hands and started praying.

"Lord Jesus, we don't know what we should be doing at this very moment, but we pray to you to guide us. Lord, we know we messed up and did not answer when you called us. Please forgive us if there is any way at all to do so. We pray that you are with us and help us to be strong during this time. Savy and I would like to get married, and we pray that you help us find someone that will do this. We will abstain from sexual sin and wait for you to help us find someone to marry us. Lord, I thank you for her. I thank you that you brought us together. I pray for your protection for us. I know your spirit is no longer restraining, but I ask that you please be with us. Help us to do your will." Savy began, "Lord, we ask that you come into our hearts." "Yes, Lord, come into our hearts," Tucker repeated. "Lord, we believe in you." "Yes, Lord, we believe that you died on the cross for our sins." "Together, we ask that you help us do the right things for you in our marriage. We want to uphold your commandments." "In your holy name. Amen."

Tucker smiled, and you could see the crinkle in his eyes. "When you know, you just know." Savy laughed and hugged him close. "In your mom's letter, she wanted me to show you where your dad's guns are." "Oh?" "Well, they are in the closet in the gun safe. I know the combination. Your dad and I used to hunt and mess around. Come on; I'll show you." Savy followed Tucker to the closet. He opened the safe and showed her the guns. "Now I'm going to have to show you how to be safe around them and how to shoot. You need to feel comfortable around a gun." "Yeah...I don't at all, but I'm not above trying." "Well, that was apparently a direct order from your dad. Carma let me know that in the letter." "What else was in that letter?" "Wouldn't you like to know..." Smiling, he picked up a handgun and two other guns that were in the safe. "Hey, there's a letter." She grabbed it out of the safe and opened it.

To Savy,

There is a key under the stairs. It goes to a hidden passage under the house. We found this passage after we had lived here about four years, when we stumbled onto a plank in the closet. So, your dad and I made it livable. We are not doomsday preppers but seeing the world and how prophecy began to look like it was unfolding before our eyes, we thought it wouldn't be a bad idea. Just in case times got hard and we had to literally go underground. This tunnel comes out inside the barn, up under the tack room floor. I think the people that sold us the house didn't even know about it. Go into the closet and count seven boards from the left going right. Lift up the seventh board. We love you and again, BE CAREFUL.

Love,

Mom and Dad

Savy looked at Tucker. "Well, we found the supplies, and that tunnel runs back to the house!" Savy said, looking at the wood floor. "Your parents were doomsday preppers, Savy!" "No, no, they weren't!" "Hey, I'm totally fine that they were!" "But Tucker, they weren't!" "Okay, okay, they were just 'prepared,'" he said using those annoying air quotes. Savy rolled her eyes and smacked his arm. "Tucker!" "If things get bad and we have to run, they won't find us. I mean, your parents didn't even know it was here for years!" He looked so impressed. "Okay! Let's go explore that tunnel they are talking about! Where's the flashlight? Did you replace the batteries?"

"One, two, three, four-" "No, Tucker, from left to right." He pulled the seventh board up. "I know, me first," Tucker said as he started going down the ladder leading underground. "Ok, Savy, you, okay?" Savy wrinkled her forehead. "Look, you're going to have to get used to it before long," Tucker said waiting for her at the bottom. She started down the ladder, and Tucker was holding both sides of her hips. She got down and faced him. He kissed her. "Tucker, here?" "Look, I couldn't help it." He turned around with the flashlight going down the tunnel. She grabbed his hand as they walked down. Finally, they came to a door, Savy handed him the key. After a bit of jiggling the key turned. "Tucker, this is crazy! This place is totally stocked!" The underground bunker seemed to have everything you would need to live during the apocalypse.

There were candles and matches already down there. He struck a match and lit a couple of candles. There was enough room for more than just the two of them down there. There were a couple of separate rooms. Savy was amazed at how big it was. One room had water stacked up by the cases and tons of food that Carma had canned. There were a few small cots, sleeping bags, and a couple of five-gallon buckets. "Hey, Savy, come here." She was checking a separate room from where Tucker was. There was a wooden door with a lock and apparently Tucker had found the key and had opened it. "Oh, wow, okay, maybe my parents were doomsday preppers, but boy, were they right. This is crazy." "Crazy good!" Tucker said with excitement. She felt her heart tug as she thought about how her parents loved her enough to do all of this. "Savy, your dad has an arsenal down here!?" He was already picking them up and looking at them. Savy's eyes got big, and she continued looking into this secret life she had no idea about. Her mom and dad had put down wood to make a floor and laid a rug in the central area with camping chairs, a card table, and a Coleman stove. There was a storage box of essentials on another small table. She picked things up, looking at all her mom had put in there. "Tucker, check this out!" He came out of the room with gear on his body. Savy looked over at him. "I don't think we are quite there yet." She laughed at him.

"You laugh now, but Savy, your parents knew what was about to go down." "I know. Look," still going through the big storage box of essentials. "Medicine, deodorant, toothpaste and toothbrushes, bars of soap, rags, and laundry detergent." They continued to look around in amazement. Tucker put everything back like it was. They followed the electrical cord out in the opposite direction. They noticed a door but couldn't push it open. "This must be where the tunnel leads to the tack room. Wow!" Tucker said. "I'll go back to the tack room tomorrow morning and try to move the boxes and find the other door."

After climbing back out of the "secret room" and stepping out of the closet back into reality, Savy went to the bathroom and splashed water on her face. She felt a little queasy after all that. It was like her heart had been racing. To think that her parents hadn't told her. They probably knew that she wouldn't have listened anyway. That she would say to them that they were irrational and "hyperfocused" on stupid things that would never come true. *I probably would have thought that they had maybe lost their minds*, she thought to herself. As she thought that her face started dripping, and her hair was a little wet. She started feeling dizzy. She hit the floor. Tucker came running over. He grabbed a wet cloth and put it over her forehead. Savy woke up slowly. "Savy, you have got to stop doing this to me." She smiled, pale as a ghost, "Tucker, I'm so sorry!" She tried to get up, and he helped her to the chair.

Tucker brought Savy some juice while she sat trying to get her bearings. "Savy, I want to get you a ring." Tucker looked at the glowing embers from the fire. "Tucker, I'm not worried about a ring. I'm more worried about us finding someone who still believes in marriage." "It's going to happen." "Look, I'm scared to leave you tonight. I don't want you passing out anymore." "Tucker, I'm fine. I honestly think it was a lot for me to take in. To think why we may have to use that space." "We will figure all this out, and it seems that your parents have done a lot already. How about I sleep on the couch tonight? I feel like you don't need to be here alone anyway." "Okay, I'm sure I'll sleep better knowing you're here." Savy kissed Tucker goodnight, he laid his gun under the couch, and Savy went to bed.

Chapter 9

Ms. Lou woke up and flung her arm out of the covers to reach for Mini and quickly felt alarmed when she wasn't there. She always woke Ms. Lou up in the mornings. She got up quickly trying to wake up. "Mini? Mini, where are you girl?" She looked frantically around the house and noticed her by the back door. She was lifeless looking. Ms. Lou reached out her hands and felt her fur. She felt stiff and cold. She began crying and Andy jumped up from the couch. He grabbed his stethoscope and listened for any sign of life, knowing that she had passed, but he wanted to give Manna Lou any amount of peace he could. "There is no heartbeat," he said looking up at his heartbroken Aunt.

She was a little shaken and Andy helped her sit down. "I will dig a spot outside for her and then we will go to Henry's," reassuring her that they were dealing with one problem at a time. She nodded her head still not believing that it was the end of little Mini's life. She went to find a little wooden box that Jack built her. She had books stored in it and thought this would be the perfect size for Mini.

When Andy was finished digging, he came in and saw the box lying beside Mini. "Manna Lou, where did you get this?" "Your uncle Jack made it for me one year for Christmas. I thought it was appropriate. She was near and dear to my heart. The best dog I've ever had." She wiped the tears from her face and smiled at Andy. "Thank you for doing this for me. I feel like there is a hole in my heart, but we have already lost everything haven't we?" Andy didn't really know what to say. They had lost every-thing, but they had to keep going. She watched as he placed Mini in the box, and followed him outside where he covered it up with dirt, and buried precious Mini in the backyard.

She was pretty quiet on the drive to Henry's and Andy turned up the news. They heard a reporter say, "They are predicting a meteor shower in five days. The biggest hit will be New Hampshire and parts of Vermont. New York is preparing for martial law soon and will have to police patrol the area. They are giving people time to get essentials and to be prepared to be in lockdown mode; now for your local forecast." "Wait, did you hear that? What's going on?" "Andy, I think we need to leave all together. This doesn't sound good at all." "No, it doesn't. Let's get to Henry since he knows we are coming now and see what his plans are." On the way, they passed military trucks and police. Ms. Lou seemed a little nervous about everything.

They got out of the car, and Henry met them. "Ms. Lou, you doin' okay this mornin'?" "No, not really. First my poor Mini passed during the night and Andy helped me bury her. And, now as we were driving here, I'm even more nervous. The whole world is being thrown into chaos. Andy and I were listening on the way here, Henry, and it doesn't sound good." "No, it doesn't. I just received a text from Savy today, and it seems she's goin' to stay in Tennessee. She has invited whoever needs help to come. I guess things are in order for her there. She explained in her text that her parents' house was left to her." They walked to the front porch and sat on the steps while Ms. Lou pulled out a cigarette. "Do you mind?" she asked, trying to be polite but knowing it was time for a cigarette. "No, you go ahead. You aren't botherin' me at all. In fact, I'll just stand over here and breathe it in as you exhale," Henry said jokingly.

Henry looked down at his phone. He read the text Savy had sent him.

I need to stay here. My parents have everything we should need. Things are quieter here for the moment. Please join us if you think you can make the journey. Delete this text and throw out your phones. I will not be reachable after this text.

"What are your thoughts, Andy? She gave me her address." "My thoughts are I don't think I have a lot to go back to. I've been looking for shelters for pets. A lot of my work hasn't come back since the 'Big Change.' I think right now, all of New York is in trouble. Just driving here out of the city limits was a challenge." "Okay, listen, we have five days to get to Tennessee, if this is what we are all decidin'. We need to get our most important things and pack up. Let's meet back here by tonight and leave first thin' in the mornin'."

Ms. Lou felt like she was living in a completely different world. She thought she was just moving in with Henry. Never did she imagine she was moving across the country. She had to wrap her head around all this, but from the sounds of it and the way the world was acting, there was no time. She grabbed the cross around her neck. It seemed that every time she felt afraid, that is what she always went to. "Jesus?" she whispered. "Help me."

"Okay, Manna Lou, let's get back and start packing our things. I had no clue that life would take a turn on us this fast, but it hasn't seemed to stop." They got back in the car and drove back to Manna Lou's.

Henry started packing bags. He started thinking about Virginia and the baby. He needed to talk to her before leaving for sure. He wouldn't be able to sleep, thinking she was left with no one and had no help. He packed all that he could and started loading his truck.

He headed down the street and knocked on Virginia's door. "Virginia, it's Henry," he called, wondering if she was afraid to come to the door. She pulled the curtain back with one hand, holding Livy in the other. She unlocked the door and invited Henry in. "Bret left," Virginia said. "What do you mean he left?" Henry asked. "He said it was too much. Livy was crying, and we were stressed out talking about the things happening. He said it was too much for him. He couldn't do it anymore." "Well, where in the heck does he think he's goin'?" Henry was mad. "He said it would be easier to go, and it's starting to make sense to him now. He said that he understood why they were taking the protocol they were taking. I don't understand. It's like they have somehow brainwashed everyone into taking this new identity so they can know where you are. Seems from everything I've been watching that maybe it would be easier, but I just can't seem to think so. That's like..." "Unconstitutional?" Henry replied. "Yes! Absolutely it is. That's what I've been thinking. Henry, are we safe?"

"Well, that's why I was droppin' by. I've been packin' everything I can. Virginia, I wouldn't be able to sleep at night knowin' there is a possibility that you are not okay. Why don't you come with me?" Virginia was puttin' the paci back in Livy's mouth. "Go with you? Where would we go?" "My friend Savy has a farm her family left for her in Tennessee, unless you're goin' to chance Bret coming back. It's totally your decision, but they are warnin' everyone that in five days when this meteor is supposed to hit, that they will declare martial law." "That's what I've been hearing too," said Virginia, "and I am not prepared at all for Livy and me to make it...just the two of us, and Bret isn't coming back."

"Tell you what, why don't you leave him a letter?" "I can write him once we are there. I've read so much on social media here lately; I smashed my phone with a hammer." "You took a hammer to your phone?" "Sure did! Trash pickup has it now. I just couldn't take a chance. Have you ever read about mama bears?" "I know they protect their cubs," Henry replied. "Yes, and I have never loved like I have loved Livy. Henry, I know God exists. I knew when she came into this world." Henry looked over at Livy. She had deep brown eyes that danced when you looked at them. "She's our number one priority." "She's mine for sure. Henry, that was it for me when he walked out on us. I told him not to come back. I honestly believe he won't. If he buys into all this, I don't think I want him to know where I live. His ideas are much too different than mine." "Well, tomorrow mornin', we are leavin' early." "I'll get packing." Henry touched her shoulder, and she patted his hand.

Henry began boarding up the windows and the back door. He wanted to keep his farm but felt that, at least for a time, he had to leave. Henry started loading up two trailers before nightfall. He had cattle in one, pigs and goats in the other, and chickens in the bed of the truck. Lazy Susy would ride in the cab. He was leaving a whole lot behind. His whole life actually. Tears welled up in Henry's eyes, looking around at the homestead. Memories flooded his mind and soul. He could see her sweeping off the porch and looking up at him, laughing.

Andy and Ms. Lou pulled up in the driveway late that night. Virginia and Livy had already brought what they needed and had fallen asleep in the spare bedroom. They stayed in the cabin on the farm. In the morning, before the sun would rise, before the roosters crowed, they would roll out of bed and get started on the road.

That morning Livy was a little fussy, not knowing what was going on, and there was no time for introductions. Andy drove one truck and trailer while Henry drove the other truck and trailer. Virginia drove her and Ms. Lou in Maggie's old car, and sweet Livy was asleep sandwiched in between luggage in the back seat. When they crossed over the bridge on their way out, each of them rolled their window down and threw their phones into the river. There was something a little more freeing, knowing that no one knows what you're doing but you. No one is even able to contact you. They were going to be living off the grid. Virginia was driving, and when Livy woke up, Ms. Lou put her paci in. "Shhh, it's okay Livy," Ms. Lou whispered softly. Virginia thought about the long drive ahead.

They drove through so much traffic and tried so hard to stick together. At times traffic was at a crawl, and they had to learn quickly not to look at others passing by. People had so much road rage and were in this panic mode of trying to take everything anyone possibly had. Andy put on his blinker to get off the interstate. They had been driving all day.

They all pulled up to a gas station and filled up. They were too scared to go to a hotel for fear of someone stealing their things. They just had to keep on driving. Andy walked up to Lou and Virginia. "Virginia, right?" "Yes, Andy, nice to finally meet you." "Thanks, and you," Virginia noticed Andy smile and look right into her eyes. Being a little shy, Virginia kept looking off but noticed his good looks. She wondered what his story was. "Are you doing okay to keep driving? I know you've got to be tired." "I can make it," Virginia responded. "Look, if we need to stop and someone watch the trucks while someone sleeps, we can do that." "No, let's just keep on. I want to get out of this mess," Virginia responded to Andy. Henry walked up. "Well, this has been pretty rough so far. Are you doin' okay?" Henry asked. "Hanging in there. I was telling Andy; I just want to keep going so we can get out of this mess." Andy glanced over at Virginia. Virginia could see him looking at her out of her peripheral vision. "I see Ms. Lou is nappin'," Henry acknowledged.

Virginia got out of the car just to stretch. She was tired, but she just wanted to keep going. "Are you sure you're okay?" Andy asked, concerned. "Yes, thank you. My back is just hurting." Virginia pushed her sunglasses up over her hair. Andy noticed her dark brown eyes. Virginia's hair was a short bleached blonde bob, and her brown roots were beginning to show. She yawned and looked back at Livy. "She's beautiful. It seems she has your eyes." Virginia smiled. "Sometimes she has her daddy's temper," she said, joking. Andy didn't know how to take that comment. "Where is he? I'm sorry I shouldn't have asked." "He left us, and it's okay, you can ask, I mean. He started believing the mess on T.V. about the New World Order. He thinks the patrolling, tracking, and lockdowns are all for the best. I feel that it infringes on people's rights."

"Absolutely it does!" Andy responded. "I'm sorry to hear all that, Virginia." "You can call me Gin and thank you. He wanted to be a part of us, but then it was like he was being pulled into two worlds. He never asked me to marry him and right now, I have to know where I stand, and I can't take any chances with Livy." "That makes total sense. It's so hard to raise a baby during this time." "Tell me about it," Gin yawned again. "Hey, I'm going in to see about getting a coffee. Would you like one?" "Yes, please," Gin replied.

She got Livy out to change her diaper in the backseat when this man came up behind her and tried to take her wallet. "I think I would drop that if I were you," Henry said, holding up his gun. The man ran off and got in his burner car and screeched his tires, taking off. Livy started crying. The noise was so loud. Virginia picked her up and held her to her chest. Andy ran out with her coffee. "What's going on?" Virginia was shaken up and could hardly speak. "I...I was changing ...Livy. He...ummm, this guy came up..." "This jerk came up tryin' to steal Virginia's wallet. So, I pulled my gun on him, and he pulled out screechin' his durn car tires. Got Livy all worked up, and I believe Gin too."

"Gin?!" Lou yelled out from the front seat, "Everything okay out there?" "Yeah... we are okay." Andy leaned up against the car with Virginia. Holding out the cup of coffee, he went to get her, "You still want to drink this? Didn't know if your heart was racing too much." "Thank you," Gin replied. "I'm okay," she said, as a tear streamed down her face. He hugged her neck because it seemed she needed it. She buried her face in his arm and was trying not to cry. "Thank you. I'm okay." "Hey, it seems Manna Lou slept through most of it. She must have her hearing aids out." "I heard that, Andy!" Virginia looked up at him wiping her tears and started chuckling at the same time. She held her coffee and took a sip. "That's good. Thank you." "No problem, I just hate I wasn't here when all that happened." "I was her knight in shinin' armor, Andy," Henry said with a smile. "Yes, you were," Gin said and hugged his neck. Henry, Andy, and Gin discussed a new route they were having to take due to so much debris and chaos. This added more to their drive, but they were getting closer. They just hoped they wouldn't run into the same issue they were trying to avoid. Andy opened her door. "Alright, you're, okay?" "I'm okay." "Andy, she's okay," Ms. Lou piped up, not knowing exactly what had just happened.

They got back on the road and Ms. Lou was wide awake. Thank God because Virginia needed something to keep her awake and keep her mind off what just happened. "My Andy is just a doll. He knows how to treat a woman, and he loves kids." Ms. Lou kept going on and on about her great nephew, and Virginia felt as though she was hinting at something. She must be trying to play matchmaker or something. "What does he do for a living?" "He is a veterinarian." It took him forever just to get accepted into the school, but he worked hard and has done well." You could tell she was proud of him. "His parents gone too?" "Yes, well, his mom and dad were raptured. Andy is an only child. They put everything they could into his education. They tried and tried to tell Andy and I all this was going to take place, but I guess, like everyone else, we thought we had time to accept." "I understand that. So, is that what you believe really happened?" "I do now," replied Lou. "Things seemed to be falling into place that support that."

Andy drove in silence for a little while. He began getting tired of the media and how they were pushing this "togetherness." He was thinking about Virginia. *Although a little younger than him, she sure was very pretty. He thought about Henry joking and saying he was her knight in shining armor and how Andy wished he had been there to be that. Who am I even kidding?* He thought. *Why would she even want me? She could still be in love with Livy's dad. Why on earth would he want to leave the both of them. That guy doesn't even realize what he had. I've spent so much of my life getting through school and building my business that I haven't even thought about God or a family. Just look where that got me. My mom tried telling me that I needed to start going to church with them on Sundays, but my excuse was that I was always too busy. Maybe I was just too lazy because Sunday was my only day to just chill. That was no excuse, though. I guess that's just worrying more about myself than any sacrifice being made. "He paid the ultimate sacrifice for you, son, and you can't give Him one day?" my mom would say. If I could do it all over, I would, but now I'm in this uncertain mess.*

Chapter 10

Savy woke up to breakfast cooking. She had a pounding headache. She wrapped her robe around her and slipped her house shoes on. "Wow, something smells good. My head is pounding." "How do you like your coffee?" Tucker asked. "One teaspoon of sugar and one tablespoon of creamer. Thank you." "You're welcome." She reached up in the cabinet and grabbed some headache medicine. Tucker put his arms around her waist and hugged her. Savy reached up and put her hand in his hair. "Okay, so I'm thinking!" Tucker released her quickly and clapped his hands together. Savy looked at him suspiciously while sipping her coffee. "Yes..." she said while looking up from her mug. "We need to practice shooting today." "Oh, I don't know, Tucker. I'm nervous, and my head is hurting this morning…" Savy grabbed a piece of bacon. "Savy, if you're worried about the shooting, you will be fine! Trust me! We are going to set up some targets and practice our aim." "If you say so. I guess I need to sooner versus later." "I even have some earmuffs for your headache. Maybe it will help." "Okay, well, I'm sure my medicine and coffee will kick in."

Tucker went to set up the targets in the field. Savy got dressed and followed him out, playing with her hair and the headgear he gave her to put on and muffle the sound of the gun firing. He brought out an AR-15 and a 9mm Glock. "So, think about the stance your legs are in when you're riding a horse. Make sure your feet are shoulder-width apart with a little bend in your knees." "Like this," Savy said, feeling a bit awkward. As Tucker was holding the 9mm, Savy was placing her feet in position. "Yes! That's it. Now take this."

Tucker then placed the handgun in her right hand. She looked at him with a serious face, trying to concentrate on what he was telling her to do. He used his hand to wrap around her hand and show her the proper position for her fingers. His arms were over her arms, trying to show her how to hold the gun. He brought her left hand up and showed her how to use it to cradle her right hand and support it. Once she had her grip down, he told her to line up the front sight post, used to align the gun and target, to the rear sights. "This is proper sight alignment, and you must maintain your sight alignment when aiming at the target. You want to aim at the center of the target." "Okay, I think I have it in sight. Now what?" "Now, slowly pull the trigger." She was so nervous, and she slowly pulled the trigger. When the gun fired off, she felt her arm move slightly over to the side. "Let's try that again, but this time gently squeeze the trigger. You want to pull more slowly," Tucker said. He watched each time until she finally started making it to the target. "I got it!" she said excitedly. "Yes, that's it!" "That wears your arms out!" she said as she put the gun down.

"With this big baby, it's the same principle with shoulder-width apart, but you're going to slide your right foot back, bend your knees and your waist, and lean forward, keeping your back straight. Get your proper sight alignment." Tucker showed her how to flip the safety off and slowly pull the trigger. He shot the first time so she would know what to expect, since it was a bigger gun. She said, "I actually feel the bigger gun is easier to manage than the handgun." "Well, I guess the AR-15 is your gun! Huh?" Tucker said, laughing in surprise. She made the best shot on that target so far. "A couple more practice shots, and you may have a bull's eye," he said. "You think so?! You think I'm good at shooting?" "I do! You're doing pretty good." "Well, I learn from the best!" Savy said, laughing. He continued to help her with little things. "Don't forget to check your alignment." As he watched her get ready for the next shot. "Breathe out slowly as you shoot."

The gun had a little bit of a kickback, which always startled Savy, but the more she practiced her shot, the more she began getting used to shooting. Savy watched Tucker shoot, and he didn't seem to miss. She watched as he practiced precisely what he had taught her. "You've had more practice than me," Savy said, feeling a little competitive. "I have," Tucker said smiling. She watched the timothy grass sway in the field as she waited on Tucker to finish up. "There seems to be a storm rolling in," as the wind continued to start blowing the grass and the trees. "Yeah, it's probably time we start back in. It does seem like it's going to rain." The raindrops started falling as they were headed back to the house.

They had made it to the porch just in time. The windows were up on the house, and Savy could hear the rain come down on the tin roof outside. She and Tucker closed the windows but left the ones on the front porch up. "I love leaving these windows up." She said as she sat on the couch, wrapping up in a blanket. Tucker laid his head on her, and they fell asleep as they listened to the rain.

Savy woke up and realized they had napped too long. "Tucker!" she yelled. "We fell asleep." He glided his hand up her thigh as they were still lying there. She looked at him, and he touched her face and kissed her. "What are we doing? We can't fall asleep!" "Well, we didn't do anything?" Tucker questioned. "Yes, but we need to be careful. I don't feel right about this until we are married." Tucker looked at Savy with those puppy dog eyes. "Alright. You're right." He got up. "I think I'm going to feed and then go home." "Well, I'm not trying to run you off," Savy said, looking at Tucker with concern in her eyes. "No, I know you're not." "Tucker, you don't have to go home. You should just bring your stuff here, and we can sleep in separate beds." "Savy, I think our parents called that shacking up, and we can't do that." "Well, it's not like anybody is here to judge us!" "Now, Savy, you know God knows, and we still have to do right in His eyes."

Savy half-smiled. He wrapped his arms around her. "Maybe we can find someone soon to marry us." She laid her head on his firm chest. His strong arms felt good around her. He kissed her head. Savy wanted to do the right thing, but a part of her wanted to do more. She tossed her hair to one side, exposing her neck. He got really close to her neck as he was talking. "I think we need to be careful. I'll tell you what. I'll be back in the morning to feed and check in on you." He kissed her neck and hugged her. Getting up he grabbed his hoodie and pulled it over his head before going outside. "I enjoyed today," he said poking his head back in the door from the outside. "I did too," she said, smiling. "Thanks for teaching me. I know I still need practice." "You did good," he said, winking at her as he closed the door.

Chapter 11

They stopped to get gas before going through Atlanta, Georgia. Henry had told them ahead of time not to make eye contact and to stay looking at the road. He had been hearing about crowd control and major military presence. The radio had reported riots and protests. There was so much unrest in the country. Henry had said, "Our main goal is to get to small-town Tennessee." *Yes,* thought Virginia. *That is all I want...to be out of this mess.* She tried not to look at what was happening around her, but it was hard to drive past all the chaos. She had her doors locked and felt herself gripping the steering wheel.

Dear God, help us make it to where we are going. I just want us to make it. Please, above all, protect my Livy.

Lou was nervous and gripping her hands. Henry and Andy tried to make a tight line so no one could squeeze between their trailers and Gin's car.

The town had buildings that were burnt to the ground, trash laying on the streets, and American flags that had been walked over and even burned. They saw a teen-ager standing all alone, crying, no one a-round to comfort him. This looked like a scene from an apocalyptic movie. Stay looking straight; she kept thinking. "NO!" Gin felt in her heart that she had to save that sweet young boy. He looked of Hispanic origin, and his tears had made a pathway down his face. "Lou...I can't leave that boy behind." Gin turned on her emergency flashers so everyone could tell she was about to stop and open her door. Andy was ahead of her and stopped the truck. Gin looked in her rearview mirror.

Henry had stopped in the line and had his gun ready. Andy jumped out, hitting the key fob quickly with his gun in the other hand. Andy said to the lost looking teenager, "Do you want to be somewhere safe?" The boy looked up dirty as can be and just pointed down the road. "Gone," he managed to say. He grabbed the boy's hand and noticed he couldn't walk, so he picked him up, unlocking the truck and he put him in the truck. At the same time Henry fired his gun, hitting a man in the shoulder who was trying to get into the driver's side of Andy's truck. Andy shut the door and ran around while holding his gun. He managed to push the guy out of the way and slammed his door. He started the truck, and they were back on the road quickly. Livy started crying, and Ms. Lou prepared her next bottle and tried propping it up with a blanket and checking on her. They tried to avoid any attention going through the big city before getting back onto the highway and tried not to draw any attention to the baby. It felt like the drive would never end. There was a lot of traffic in Atlanta and a lot of people.

Gin was thinking that it seemed people were outraged these days and easily offended. She, like many others, felt that when you had to go into a grocery store, you didn't even want to smile at someone. They may take a smile wrong, but if you didn't smile, they might also take that wrong. Everything had changed so fast. It seemed best to stay home more and not deal with people in these crazy times. Gin wondered if this Savy would be okay with a baby coming in on the scene. Henry would take up for Livy. He really loved her. *How can I give her the same upbringing I had?* thought Virginia. *It will be impossible these days to give a child the same up-bringing. I used to stay outside till my mother called me in during the summer-time. I know I will never let Livy out of my sight. Not in this day and time. I have this precious jewel I was given. She's beautiful, and I will go mama bear if I have to.*

Gin thought to herself, I just saw *someone hit the side of Andy's truck up ahead of me, and Andy just kept going. He never let up. It was like Andy felt the same way I did when I saw that boy. He was already stopping no sooner than I had turned my flashers on. I know we can't save the world, but that would've been another haunting.* "What's on your mind?" Ms. Lou asked. "Well, I am still in an amazement that Andy and I were both seeing that sad boy." "Andy has always had a softness to him. I can't count the times that boy has brought home stray animals! I know before everything changed; he had told me he wished he had a family. I told him he has been successful and focused on his business. Now I know his heart has been thinking about what if." Gin just listened to Ms. Lou talk and go on and on about how softhearted Andy was. How, on the outside, he may seem different, but he had a huge heart.

Henry was in a dead stare straight ahead. He couldn't take his eyes off the line. At times they were dodging trash, bodies, grocery carts, and cars stopped mid-road. Henry would get his truck out first, allowing Gin and Andy to get in front to keep the line together. He patted Lazy

Susy's head. She lay right beside him and his gun, with her head down. "Why didn't I listen to Maggie all those years?" "Why couldn't I have just accepted?" Lazy Susy's eyes would blink from side to side as she listened. "I'm tryin' to focus on the now. That's all we've got, now."

Finally, they got outside of Atlanta. "We won't be too much further now. I know you are upset. I've never seen anything like this." The boy sat quietly, not talking at all. "I'm sorry this is happening." He looked about eighteen. He just stared out the window for the next couple of hours.

Andy kept thinking about Gin and how she was feeling after everything had happened at the gas station. How was it that all this time, even before the "Big Change," he never really had a lady catch his eye? How was it that now in the midst of chaos, he couldn't stop thinking about Gin? Her bleached blonde hair was a little wavy pulled back in a little nub with some falling out of the bobby pins. Even when she had her hair up and messy, she still looked classy somehow. The silver hoops in her ears, and her neck showing, made Andy feel crazy. I've got to get my mind off of her, he thought. Tennessee. We are getting closer, thought Andy.

"Is there any water?" The boy finally spoke. "Behind the seat, there is a little cooler. Look in there and get you something." The boy reached behind and pulled out a water. Taking a drink, he looked at Andy. "My mom was just gone one day. She was just gone." With tears in his eyes, he continued "I'm not sure why you stopped, but I had been walking and praying to myself. I asked God if He was real to please help me. It didn't happen immediately. I had been with the wrong guys. My mom warned me about the kids I was hanging out with, but I didn't listen. I guess I knew it all along." "As every boy your age does," responded Andy.

"Look, everyone who left has mentioned one common indicator in all of this. The Lord took them." "How do you know?" the boy looked at Andy, questioning him. "Some had written notes; some claimed their loved ones kept talking about the rapture. There seems to be a complete split in ideas. They either believe fully now because of the scriptures or have fallen into this new world idea."

"Well, what do you mean? I mean, do you believe in aliens?" the boy asked. "I believe if we start seeing some crazy things, it might be Satan himself or the fallen angels. This new world idea seems to have people thinking that all people are actually worshipping the same god, that they own nothing due to government control, and that being nice to the earth is what is really important, so much so that it controls our lives. They create this fear of an unbalanced atmosphere. So where are those friends you were hanging with?"

"They went to rob a drugstore, and I just started running in the other direction. There were other times when I was trying to get away from them, but by that time, they had guns. When they were finally distracted, I ran." "Some friends, man." "I know," he hung his head. "I fell, and I think I messed my leg up." Andy looked down and saw his leg was bleeding. "Pull your jeans up to your knee." "How long has it been like that?" "A couple of days."

Andy pulled off on the next exit, and the others followed. The cars seemed to be fewer and fewer. "I'm going to clean your leg. If you are not careful, you will have an infection set up in your leg." Andy had a medical kit behind the seat. He opened his door and had him lay his leg on Andy's knee. Andy rinsed the wound with alcohol. "I've got to get a piece of glass out." "What!? How deep?" "Listen, kid, do you want your leg to get better?"

Henry walked up, "Everythin' ok?" "He's gotta dig glass out of my leg!" "I'd let him do it. He knows what he's doin'." "What is he, a doctor or something?" "Somethin' like that." The boy furrowed his brow. "OK, just do it." Henry gave him a swig of whiskey, and Andy started to get the glass out.

Virginia was getting Livy out of her car seat. "She's so tired of being in this car. I know we are almost there, but I'm so tired." Virginia stretched her legs while holding Livy. Henry was walking back to his truck with a bottle of whisky. "Henry, is everything alright?" He held up his bottle, "Medicinal purposes only!"

Virginia gave Livy to Lou and walked up to Andy's truck. "He ok?" "We stopped to clean out his leg." As he was wrapping the bandage around, the boy looked up at Gin. He was sweaty, and his lips looked a bit pale. "Andy, I think he needs to rest," Andy smirked at her. "I think you need to rest." "Coffee only goes so far, but I can keep going. I know we are almost there. It has taken us almost twice the amount of time to get to Tennessee than it usually does," Gin said tiredly. "We didn't have much of a choice. Henry looked at the map to reroute us and we had to go south to avoid damage." "I have been following you guys. Let's just keep moving," Andy said.

Andy looked up at her. "Can you?" "I can." Andy loaded up his medical supplies. "It's still about four hours." "What's four more hours? Right?" She turned to walk back to the car, but he grabbed her hand.

She looked down at her hand. "I'm sorry. I just wanted to tell you. You're a brave mom for Livy. She's lucky to have you." Blushing a bit, "I don't know that anybody is lucky to live through this. What was I thinking bringing a baby into the world?" "Gin, not many people were thinking." "If I could've kept her inside the womb, I think I would've." "You're doing the best you can." She laid her hand on his shoulder. "Thank you for your kind words. That means a lot to me, Andy." He watched her walk the rest of the way to the car and noticed her waist. He quickly looked away when his Aunt Lou caught his eye. "Okay, let's load up!" Andy slammed the truck door and loaded back up.

"I noticed that conversation," Ms. Lou mentioned. Gin blushed from the neck down. "Well, I...Andy is very nice," she ended while pulling on her seat belt. "If I didn't know any better, I would think you had feelings for my Andy." "Feelings? I just ended things with my last boyfriend. I can't have feelings for him." "Sure, you can. I'm not saying that you can't have feelings for what used to be. But honey, that's not even a thing anymore. You can only look forward, and I would say it seems to me that you don't want to admit that you're looking forward." Virginia looked straight ahead and turned and looked at Ms. Lou. She threw her head back, "Is that right?" "I'm not ignorant, that's for sure!" "Well, Ms. Lou, he is mighty fine, but the world is ending." "Honey, God made man a comparable mate, and I think even if the world is ending it doesn't mean you can't love." Gin blushing a bit, didn't know how this woman could be so forward with her, but then again, older women seem to make no bones about it. She obviously saw the way they were looking at each other. *I wonder if Andy felt anything.*

Chapter 12

Savy and Tucker had been getting water from the nearby creek and filtering it. She carried two five-gallon buckets back to the house, Tucker carrying his buckets behind her. They had been trying to get everything ready in case they had company arrive. She didn't know if Henry had ever gotten her text, but she and Tucker had decided to try and be overly prepared. She had gotten pretty good with a gun, practicing with Tucker. She had gotten used to having him around. She felt free around him. Maybe she felt free that she was out in the country. Even amid everything, she had still been able to laugh a little.

That same night Tucker had to read her scripture until she drifted off to a half-asleep, half-awake state. His gentle voice made her calmer. Tucker didn't know much scripture, just what her dad would give him from time to time working on the farm, but he had regrets about not listening better. Every knee would bow, every tongue would confess. He knew that now. Crazy how it had to take some supernatural event before he would ever really listen, and now here they were, readying themselves for what else the scriptures told. Revelation is a hard book to understand, but after hearing of the coming meteors, there had to be something literal to it too. Savy drifted off while he was reading her mother's Bible to her. Psalm 63:3-5 (NKJV) was highlighted in blue.

> Because Your lovingkindness *is* better than life, My lips shall praise You. Thus I will bless You while I live; I will lift my hands in Your name. My soul shall be satisfied as with marrow and fatness, And my mouth shall praise *You* with joyful lips.

Savy suddenly awoke out of sleep, breathing really hard. She sat up and all of a sudden passed out. "Are you ok?" Tucker asked. "Savy, breathe. You have to breathe. Look at me." He touched her chin and lifted it to look into her eyes. "I can't. I can't. Breathe. I'm scared." "I'm scared too. It's ok. Savy, it's ok to be scared." Cupping her face with both hands, he looked at her. "Savy, we have to be strong. Listen, listen to my voice Savy. Take one long breath and hold it. Now breathe out." She kept trying to listen, but she felt dizzy.

She could hear seagulls and the ocean. Her mom was picking up seashells with a straw hat on. Savy was running through the waves. She was a child. The sand was beneath her feet. She ran up and grabbed her mom's hand. It felt right. She started laughing and squeezed her hand twice. Her mom squeezed it back twice. She looked up, and her mom placed her hand on Savy's face.

Savy blinked her eyes awake. Tucker had a rag on her forehead and was patting her cheek. The tea kettle was whistling. "I'm making you some tea. You passed out." Savy felt clammy.

He ran into the kitchen to plop the tea bag in and cut the eye on the stovetop off. As Savy was resting on the couch Tucker filtered through the rest of the water from the creek. She calmed down holding her warm mug. She could hear the rain coming down outside and looked out the window while sipping on her tea. She watched as each raindrop fell into a puddle by the window and made ripples. "It's amazing how each raindrop causes so much destruction inside calm waters." "Much like our lives, I guess. Sometimes everything is calm, and then the floodgates open," Tucker said, sitting down beside her. "I'm sorry-" "Hey, no, don't be sorry. There is nothing to be sorry about. Trust me, in all this, I've had my freakout moments." "Really, when?" "It's happened," Tucker protested.

"Savy, I'm here. It's not going to be easy." Leroy began howling at headlights coming up the driveway. "Stay here, Savy." "That's three vehicles." Tucker grabbed his gun. Savy stayed inside. He locked the front door and went out the back to see what was happening. He heard cattle. The vehicles' doors shut, and he could hear a baby. He walked around with his gun by his side. Savy could hear Henry's voice. She slid her muck boots on and went out the back. "Tucker," Savy whispered. "It's ok. It's Henry."

Savy and Tucker walked around the house. Leroy began sniffing and must've found Lazy Susy's scent on Henry. "I didn't know if you were going to come!" Savy said, hugging Henry's neck. "Leroy is our hunting dog. He has the nose of a blood hound." Henry chuckled and bent down to pet him after letting him sniff his hands. "Well, he will get along just fine with my Bassett." He opened the door of his truck and let them get acquainted. "Whew! We made it. I didn't know if we would. It's been quite the journey. I brought some friends with me," Henry looked back, shrugging to Savy. "I see that." "I hope that's not going to be a problem." "Henry, one thing I'm learning is, it's not about me." Henry gave a half-smile and a nod. "Oh! This is my...this is..." "-Tucker," he said, holding out his hand firmly, feeling that Henry was somewhat of a father figure. "Well, it's nice to meet you, Tucker." Henry pointed, "this here is Andy and..." Andy came up to shake hands. "That's Mateo," Andy said. "So, I guess you had words then?" Henry asked. "Yes sir, he gave in after I dug into his leg," Andy replied, almost whispering. Ms. Lou was helping Virginia get some diapers out. Savy walked over to Gin and the baby. "And who do we have here?" she asked. "This is Livy, and I am Virginia. You can call me Gin if you'd like." She glanced up after changing Livy's diaper. "Look," Gin said, as she was picking Livy back up. "I know babies aren't quiet, but we had nowhere else to go. They are mentioning astronomical events that I can't even imagine. I hope we won't be a problem for you." Savy looked at Gin's face. She could tell that she was holding back tears. "I know y'all must've seen a lot as you have made such a journey. We are going to experience things we have never experienced. You're here. We are going to stay together. I think we all have a lot to learn." "Let's get everybody inside. I know y'all are tired." Savy grabbed the baby's bag for Virginia.

Savy started baking fresh biscuits and eggs as the men put the livestock up. Lazy Susy had found her spot on the floor with her big, long ears spread out on the cold hardwood. "Now, I know we won't be able to eat like this much considering food rationing, but I felt like this was a special occasion." "It feels like we just drove through scenes of an apocalyptic movie," Gin said as she shut the door gently from putting the baby down to sleep. "I know it's terrible, and it's only going to continue to get worse. There is nothing we can do about it but be here together and enjoy the few times we may be able to laugh." "I may have to laugh to keep from crying," Gin said. Lou sat in an old rocking chair in the kitchen with her head laid back. "I think she is exhausted," Gin said as she grabbed a blanket and put it over her.

The boys came through the door taking their boots off. Tucker came up behind Savy and put his arms around her waist, his nose nuzzled against her neck. "I've got biscuits in the oven." "It's been a while since we've eaten. My belly's been thinkin' my throat's been cut," Henry said with a grin on his face. Andy looked over at Gin, "is Livy asleep?" "I just laid her down." "So, how was the drive?" Savy asked, looking over at Mateo, noticing he was very quiet.

"It's been a long hard drive," Andy replied. "We noticed that once we came closer and closer to Tennessee, we seemed to be out of danger zones. People were just grabbing car doors and trying to steal cars at gunpoint. I've honestly never seen anything like it," Gin said, as she sat on the floor with her head in her hands. "It's only a matter of time before it reaches us," Henry said. "How do you have an oven? We noticed that most of the houses are completely dark," Gin asked. "Generator," Tucker replied. "There is a lot we need to talk about," Savy said as she put biscuits on the counter. "But let's just enjoy this moment of being together. It's been a long day for everybody."

Mateo reached for the Bible that Henry unpacked from his bag. "May I?" he asked. "Of course. Matthew is a good book if you want to start there," Henry said gladly. He began reading most of the night while people were catching up talking.

Matthew 17:1-4 (NJKV)

> Now after six days Jesus took Peter, James, and John his brother, led them up on a high mountain by themselves; and He was transfigured before them. His face shone like the sun, and His clothes became as white as light. And behold Moses and Elijah appeared to them, talking with Him. Then Peter answered and said to Jesus, "Lord, it is good for us to be here; if You wish, let us make here three tabernacles: one for You, one for Moses, and one for Elijah."

Henry could tell the Lord was doing a work in Mateo's heart. He saw that he was reading Matthew 17. "Ahhh the trans-figuration," Henry said. "I remember this sermon. Me and Maggie talked about how Peter wanted to stay. You see, he didn't want to come off the mountain. He just got through seein' the most beautiful scene he had ever seen in his life, and he didn't want to leave." Mateo nodded listening to Henry. "He wanted to build tabernacles and see; we can't live on the mountain top. We have to come back down in the valley. We are to show people the way to Jesus. It's hard in the valley, but He never told us it was going to be easy." "How were you lost? How were you not taken?" Mateo said confused. "I was too stubborn to listen," Henry said. "I guess I have always been that person that needs to be hit upside the head before I listen." "I want to accept Christ," Mateo said to Henry. "I believe the Lord sent me you and all these nice people." "Well, Mateo the Lord doesn't say you have to know everythin'. He says believe in Me. Do you think you can do that? Do you think you're ready to be saved? The only way is to accept Jesus as your Lord and Savior." "Yes sir, I'm ready," Mateo responded. They prayed a prayer together and joined everyone else at the table. They broke bread and enjoyed the night.

Part 2 –

Mid-Tribulation

Matthew 24:9 (NKJV)

"Then they will deliver you up to tribulation and kill you, and you will be hated by all nations for My name's sake."

As 3 ½ years had passed they all worked together to make sure they were as prepared as they could be. Closer to the end of the 3 ½ years it became harder and harder to find supplies. Violence ensued in every direction. The best thing to do was stay away from people, or big populations. They had learned to live off the land and not take anything for granted. Livy knew nothing different. She has been growing up in a world where there isn't an abundance. They have developed a strong love and would do anything for one another. There was a darkness that began to linger. People became more offended, hostile, and violent, even more so than when all this began. Governmental control was oppresssive and highly volatile. Camps were being set up to reprogram the population and oppose Christianity.

Revelation 13:11-18 (NKJV)

Then I saw another beast coming up out of the earth, and he had two horns like a lamb and spoke like a dragon.

And he exercises all the authority of the first beast in his presence, and causes the earth and those who dwell in it to worship the first beast, whose deadly wound was healed.

He performs great signs, so that he even makes fire come down from Heaven on the earth in the sight of men.

And he deceives those who dwell on the earth by those signs which he was granted to do in the sight of the beast, telling those who dwell on the earth to make an image to the beast who was wounded by the sword and lived.

He was granted *power* to give breath to the image of the beast, that the image of the beast should both speak and cause as many as would not worship the image of the beast to be killed.

He causes all, both small and great, rich and poor, free and slave, to receive a mark on their right hand or on their foreheads,

And that no one may buy or sell except one who has the mark or the name of the beast, or the number of his name.

Here is wisdom. Let him who has understanding calculate the number of the beast, for it is the number of a man: His number *is* 666.

Chapter 13

Savy lay there watching ash fall from the sky. Her ears were ringing. She felt like she couldn't move. She heard faint screaming. She managed to roll over and crawl to her. She was cold and crying. She knew she had to try to make it. As she started toward Livy, she realized her right leg was bleeding. She got to her, still lying there, but wrapping her arms around her. "Listen," Savy managed to get out of her scratchy voice. "I've got you. Safs got you. Shhh. Please try to be quiet. Shhhh." She sat up with Livy. She got to her feet and ran for cover, not knowing what she would find next. Not knowing how long she had been out. She heard footsteps, and Savy held her close, whispering in her ears.

"I've got you," she repeated in her ear. "Listen and do what I do and exactly as I say." Livy looked scared and in a state of shock.

If she could make it to the tree line, she could try and get back to the bunker. There was a stillness in the air, but she knew someone was close. She tried to wait until the footsteps she heard sounded closer. She took off running with Livy, feeling the pain in her leg, but not having a choice. She had to run for their lives. She heard a shot and started running faster. Knowing she had to get him off their back, but unsure what to do next. She could feel her heart pounding in her chest. The bullet hit the tree, and she began to run faster, gripping Livy tighter. Her breathing was becoming deeper, but she was trying to control it. She heard another shot.

"Savy! Savy!" She continued to run. He was gaining on them, and she tripped and fell. Tucker pulled his gun, put his sight on him, and pulled the trigger. The man went down. "Hey, it's okay." He bent down to the ground and pulled her and

Livy close to him. Savy felt like she had the breath knocked out of her and she began to sob desperately. "I don't remember what happened. I just woke up and knew I had to protect her." Tears were streaming down her face. Tucker wrapped his arms around her squeezing her tight, feeling that she was all he had left. "We've got to get back to the bunker." Further out than they wanted to be, Tucker helped Savy to her feet, and put her arm around his shoulders to lean on him as they hobbled back. "Listen for others and try to be quiet," Tucker said to Livy. Finally, they came to the tack room and pulled the floor up and started down the ladder into the tunnel. "Saf, I'm scared." Livy cried inside the tunnel. Tucker was behind them to make sure everything was safe. Savy turned to Livy, "I know Livy. I am too. We have to remember that there is something bigger than what we are living for." Livy cried, "I'm not feeling too good." "Come on, let's just get home."

As soon as they got to the bunker, Tucker grabbed a five-gallon bucket, and

Livy started vomiting into it. Savy was holding back her hair. "I think it's nerves," Savy said looking up at Tucker. "You need to try and get some rest tonight. You've got to be exhausted." "I should've never gone that far. I should've been more careful." Tucker put his hands up to her mouth. Pointing to the other room as Savy helped get Livy comfortable on a pallet. Tucker grabbed the bandages out of the first aid kit. He began to clean Savy's leg and wrap it. "Do you think anybody noticed us after we were close to home?" Savy said nervously. "I just don't remember much before. I know we went looking for some food, and it felt so good to be out. I thought we were ok. Livy was begging Gin to go with me. She wanted to go outside. Gin let her and I feel that I have destroyed her trust."

"Hey," Tucker said, grabbing her hand. "Another meteor hit, you can't help that, and the guy I shot, he was with the United Nations. He must've spotted y'all when you ran. I thought you had been gone for too long. I decided to take the route I knew you would've taken." "I'm so glad you did. I'm so sorry Tucker. What if something would've happened to Livy? I would've never forgiven myself." "But it didn't," he paused looking at her. "I know we are having to figure out all of this. We know there is no guarantee that we will even make it, but we have to focus on God and each other. He is the only thing that matters. That's clear."

"I'm so scared." "I know." Tucker hugged Savy close. He could feel her tremble. "If we die, we gain Christ," Tucker whispered in her ear. "If I die first, I'll be waiting for you there." Savy shook her head and tried to gain her composure to go check on Livy. She was asleep. Savy knelt down to kiss her forehead. She looked at Tucker concerned. Her head seemed hot to the touch. Tucker then felt her head. "I'm going to stay up with her while you get some rest," Tucker said, tucking her hair behind her ear. Feeling bad for Livy, Savy responded. "I'm going to sleep on the other side of her. I'm sure Gin will be back shortly."

He knelt down beside Livy and prayed putting his hand on Livy's back.

"Dear Lord,

I know that we are here because of our disobedient hearts, but I ask that you please be with Livy. Help her to feel better come morning. She's tired and nervous. I pray that this is not something too serious, and that you please provide the means that we need. Lord you are powerful and mighty. You are the true, living, and only God. Lord, we thank you for shelter tonight in your precious name.

A-men."

Ms. Lou had been asleep in the other room. She got to her feet slowly and saw Savy, Tucker, and Livy laying down. She noticed vomit in the bucket beside them and went to rinse it out. Gently she took a blanket she had made and draped it over sweet Livy. She decided to make a little broth to hopefully settle Livy's stomach. She had always kept the bones from the chickens to help make broth for times like this. As she waited on the broth, she opened up her Bible.

Proverbs 24:1-6 (NKJV)

Do not be envious of evil men, nor desire to be with them; for their heart devises violence, and their lips talk of troublemaking. Through wisdom a house is built, and by understanding it is established; By knowledge the rooms are filled With all precious and pleasant riches. A wise man *is* strong, Yes, a man of knowledge increases strength; For by wise counsel you will wage your own war, and in a multitude of counselors *there is* safety.

"Lord, help me to build my house on the wisdom that you give me. Help me to be strong and to not desire the evil desires of this world. I pray that I can finish this with you," she whispered.

An hour had passed, and Tucker heard someone coming in the tunnel. The key was turning the doorknob. It was Henry.

He had brought in some more milk from the cows.

Savy woke up. Livy was asleep on the floor in between Savy and Tucker, who had stayed awake watching Livy. They slowly got to their feet and noticed Henry was a little shook up as well. Savy took his hand and led him over to the storage room. "Things got bad quickly." "You can say that again," Henry replied. "I thought Gin would be back already," Savy said concerned. "It's becomin' like a war zone out there. I managed to get some of the animals fed, but I'm scared it's just a matter of time before they find out we are here." They had moved the animals more into the woods on the property to be less noticeable. Ms. Lou poured some soup so it could be cooling down for when Livy woke up. She shuffled over to Savy and kissed her forehead. "May God be with us," she whispered.

Gin and Andy came in dirty as ever. Savy rushed and hugged them. "We were worried sick! Wait, where is Mateo?" Gin and Andy looked at each other. "How are we to keep doing this?" "We ended up hiding in the mud because there was a soldier. He's gone," Gin cried. Andy punched the wall. He was upset and mad at himself. "There was no way, or we would have been shot too. I was trying to keep Gin safe," Andy said exasperated. "Mateo took off running and the soldier took him down with one shot," Gin said nervously. "I managed to get back to Mateo after the soldier left. There was no pulse. I put my ear to his chest and there was no heartbeat." Andy began to cry, but there was an anger that he couldn't shut off. "I will not run again. They will have to kill me," he said furiously.

"We tried to wash off, but it is dried and caked onto our skin...it was hard to get it all." Savy grabbed a bucket of water and a rag with a sliver of soap. "Thank you," Gin replied. She broke down in tears, and Savy grabbed her hand and squeezed. "You have to be strong. I'm not doing a very good job either, but we must." Gin's breathing became rapid, and then turned into quiet jerking sobs as she was trying to hold it in. Then she wailed out not catching her breath. Savy grabbed her other hand and looked at her with a worried brow, and a hurt in her expression. Gin looked at her eyes. "It's so hard to be strong in a time when everything is gone and falling apart at the seams." "He laid there lifeless looking at me as the rain pelted him on his face. That's all I can see. His lifeless expression. How do I go on from this?" "This world is not our home," Savy said, reassuring Gin that there was something bigger.

"Livy is running a fever," Savy told Gin making sure that she knew, but also scared of her reaction. Gin pulled Livy's body into her arms and began waking her up. "Let's see if you can keep a little soup down." Livy looked weak in her eyes. "Momma, me and Saf ran, and I was scared." Gin swept the hair out of her face and kissed her cheek cradling her. "We are all scared at times Livy," Gin replied with swollen eyes. Her head hurt so bad it felt like a shock kept pounding through her brain. Gin squeezed her tight. The very thought of not being able to go on without her shook her to her core. She kissed her over and over. "I'm so sorry," Savy said feeling terrible. "This isn't anyone's fault. I let her go. If she wasn't with you, she would have been with me. You did exactly what I would have done. You protected her with your life." "Momma, Saf and Tuck saved me." "I know baby. I'm so sorry this happened to you. Let's try and stay in for a while. At least until things hopefully die down out there." She looked up at Savy with a helpless look. They were all weary from the day, and not a one of them had the energy to fight or be upset, but just to be silent.

"There is a time for everything. Did you know the Bible tells us that?" Gin opened up Maggie's Bible. "This is what we have to cling to, or we could lose our minds."

Ecclesiastes 3:1-8 (NJKV)

To everything *there is* a season,
A time for every purpose under heaven:
A time to be born,

And a time to die;
A time to plant,
And a time to pluck *what is* planted;
A time to kill,
And a time to heal;
A time to break down,
And a time to build up;
A time to weep,
And a time to laugh;
A time to mourn,
And a time to dance;
A time to cast away stones,
And a time to gather stones;
A time to embrace,
And a time to refrain from embracing;
A time to gain,
And a time to lose;
A time to keep,
And a time to throw away;
A time to tear,
And a time to sew;
A time to keep silence,
And a time to speak;
A time to love,
And a time to hate;
A time of war,
And a time of peace.

Chapter 14

Jules had left her grandfather in peace. His body could not make it anymore. In a time that has been so incredibly chaotic, she did not feel sad, but more relieved that he didn't have to go through any more of this. She knew he went to meet his Maker. She held his hand as he took his last breath and drifted off. She took his necklace off his neck and put it around hers. She packed her bag grabbing some pictures of her childhood and her grandfather's Bible. They had been reading scripture every morning to be able to get through the days. She grabbed beef jerky that they had dried out and a can filled with water.

There were things she had learned while staying with her grandfather, and if it hadn't been for him, she wouldn't have known how to survive. He was tough and came from a different generation. A generation that had to work hard. He worked so hard his hands had calluses on them. He knew how to have very little and still be happy. They grew some crops, and he taught her how to can and keep things back. He said this was being smart knowing that a famine was coming. She grabbed a few cans and stuffed them in her backpack. She put her hand over her grandfather's once more and left. She didn't know what to do since it was only her. She knew she had to get to Savy.

She had to take the woods. Trucks were coming into Nashville, and she knew it would only be a matter of time before they would get closer. She had heard rumors of soldiers being around, and she knew they were trying their best to control everyone. These were not the soldiers that Jules grew to know and love that held a patriotic stance for the America that she and many had once loved. No, these soldiers were of one world. Not all spoke English.

The news had been showing a meteor that hit close to Savy's, but she couldn't give up on her. They had been friends since elementary school, and she needed to make sure she was okay. Never would she imagine when they left New York that this much would have happened. She saw Savy a few years ago and loaded her up with canned goods, while Savy gave her fresh milk and some eggs. Savy had told her about the storage room her parents had stocked and told Jules if she ever needed to, she was welcome to join Savy, Tucker, and the others. She hugged her tight and said, "We've got this girl! I'll see you." She remembered watching her and Tucker drive off in the truck. They had tried to get her to come with them, but her grandfather refused to leave, and she wouldn't leave him. Now she was willing to make the hike. She took a deep breath in as she hiked through the trees. She smelled the sweet fragrance of the outdoors. Jules walked all day, and it began to get dark. Grabbing her hammock out of her backpack, she tied it to two trees. Jules had gathered some wood and started a small fire. She warmed herself up and ate some jerky.

She had fallen asleep and woke up to the sound of someone close by. She tried to be quiet and slowly rolled out of the hammock. She tried to untie her hammock in the dark and started walking quietly. Jules could hear them and wondered what kind of people they were. She didn't want to bring another person with her to Savy's, especially not knowing them. She continued to walk and heard them say, "Do you hear something?" Jules stopped midtrack behind a tree.

"Shhh..." "There is nobody. You're just drunk!" "I did to hear someone! Well, I thought I did." "You thought you heard someone...you're drunk! Well, what are you going to do now that you have no more? Huh?" He started laughing at his drunk friend but was also disgusted. "No wonder you were left, you can't even pull your head out of your ass and deal with what we have been dealt. I mean you think you're a man?" Jules was so quiet listening to them argue and all of the sudden she heard one of them punch the other. She felt flush, not knowing who these people were. She was scared but also started thinking about a game plan on what she would need to do if she was discovered. She had pepper spray and a gun if she had to use it. She could tell the drunk guy won.

"Hey," he yelled out looking at her. She took off running. "Hey! I knew I heard someone." He tried to run and then ran straight into a tree. She turned and looked, and he was knocked out, but the other guy was up. She held out her gun. "Don't you dare try anything," she said holding her gun toward them. He held his hands up serious. "Hey, miss, I'm not going to try anything. Then stay there and I'm going to walk away and if you follow me, I'm going to shoot." She began to walk backwards still holding the gun towards him until she had enough distance between her and them.

The other guy, who had been knocked out for the rest of the night, started to wake up slowly. He sat up and felt blood on his forehead. "Take a drink," his buddy said, holding up a canister of water to him. "Where did you get this?" "You were right. The girl had it and left it behind. Sorry, I didn't believe you and called you a drunk."

"She was beautiful," Landon said as he was drinking the water and washing off his forehead with the water. "Yeah, well you can forget about her because I don't think anybody is getting close to her. She held her own and had a gun on her." "Well, Tate what do you expect? Two guys and one girl? I was not in my right mind. I'm sure she thought we were bad news. I can't deal with all this. You're right, Tate. I deserve all this." "Look man we all deserve this. I was just mad that you were drunk last night. Nobody wants to be going through any of this, but we are. Now today we need to try and find some food."

As they marched forward trying to find food, Landon felt weary...but at the same time his heart pounded for the first time in a long time after seeing her. It had been over three years since the "Big Change," and he had been living in the past. Not wanting to even move forward. He wanted to just lay down at times and give up. His life was no good anymore. This was more than he could bare, but last night when he saw her...there was something. Landon missed his wife, and no one could ever live up to his family, but they were gone, and he was here. Even though there was an energy about him as he couldn't get his mind off of her, there was a feeling of guilt. He couldn't possibly allow himself to be happy after being left without his family. They were his life, but how could he continue here on this earth without love?

The two began to hear big loud explosions. Without even saying a word they grabbed their bags and began to run. They ran like their lives depended on it. Fire falling from the sky. More meteors were falling, and the sun darkened as if it were midnight.

Chapter 15

The ground was shaking, and the lights flickered above their heads as more meteors fell. They were all huddled together in the tiny bunker. Livy had her head buried in Gin's chest, while, Lazy Susy had her head resting on Livy's legs. The dog seemed to sense Livy's need for a friend. She had been through so much. Filled with exhaustion, everyone had been silent for the last hour. Tucker thought to himself, the gnawing pain in my stomach has finally subsided, and he laid his head back against the wall.

His mind focused on Savy and her wavy dark hair hitting her skin. She had a way of making him love her more and more every day. *They were married not long after Henry showed up. He remembered their wedding; they made the farm look quaint. Jules, Gin, and Lou decorated the yard in front of an old oak tree on the farm. There was simplicity and a relaxed feeling at that moment. Even though so much had changed they were able to enjoy that small moment in time. Savy wore her mom's old wedding dress. The dress was solid white with lace sleeves, showing her back coming down in a V-shape and buttons from the small of her back down. She looked perfect. Our only wish would have been for our families to have been able to see her walk down the aisle. Scott would have loved to have given her away. Henry walked her down and then officiated the ceremony for us. She was so nervous as she held my hands. I knew I wanted to be with Savy forever and she still talks about my hands being steady as a rock. Savy's head laid over on my shoulder and I drifted off thinking about dancing at our wedding. Her hips fit so closely to mine with her head lying on my shoulder feeling her breath on my neck. As our body's seemed tied together indefinitely, we swayed to the music coming from Andy's guitar. She smelled of a sweet perfume. I knew that night was going to be in my memory forever.*

"Tucker, I'm fine. Just live for Him. He is all that matters. I've seen Him Tucker. I have seen Jesus." She was in a field of daisies laughing and singing with his niece. She smiled really big with laughter. There was happiness there. It was bright and the wind blew his niece's hair. She laughed, "Tucker, I love-"

"Tucker! Hey..." she said softly trying to wake him. She fingered through his hair and kissed his face. "Tucker are you okay?" He cracked his eyes open sleepily, "I...I saw my sister and my niece." "What?" Savy looking at him with wonder. "Yeah...she said she saw Jesus." "Maybe God gave you that," Savy replied. "She said, live for Him. He is all that matters." Savy sat up and wrapped her arms around his neck. Pressing her face against his neck she could feel her throat swelling as she swallowed hard holding back tears herself. He lay his head on her chest with tears in his eyes. *Sometimes it felt as if we were just surviving and, at those times, we wished so bad for all this to be over. For the seven years to be over. Will we survive all this?* Tucker thought.

He was too tired to explain his dream or the thoughts that ran through his mind, and honestly Savy was too tired to talk. Filled with only the deep love they had for each other they laid there without any explanation and were okay with the quietness of the bunker and just holding each other.

Gin and Andy grabbed some rice that was already cooked and put some chicken broth on top and started serving. It was cold, but they had learned to eat what was given. They ate by candlelight and flash-lights. In normal times, this could sound very romantic, but in survival mood it was anything but. "Manna, Livy spoke up. Can I sit beside you?" "Well absolutely sweetie! You can always sit by me." Livy stood up and walked towards Lou. She plopped down hard and snuggled in close. Ms. Lou had found a love for Livy. She thought she couldn't possibly have any more love in her heart for another child besides her own children and grandchildren, but Livy had pushed her way through the cracks of Lou's heart. Livy brought some laughter, love, innocence, and many times entertainment. She was like a tiny grown up. She had never really been around any other kids her own age before.

"Where's Mateo?" Livy asked. Gin glanced up and went immediately over to Livy. "Livy, you know how mommy has told you about Jesus and how a lot of people went to go be with Him before you were even born?" Livy looked confused. "Yes momma, and all the kids will be able to pet all the animals?" "Yes, well he went to meet Jesus and be in Heaven with Him." "So, he is waiting for us?" "Well, he is probably pretty busy, but yes, he will be there waiting for us." Her eyes filled with tears. "I wasn't ready though mommy." "I know," Gin replied. "I wasn't either." She grabbed Livy and saw his face as she closed her eyes. "Let's pray," Henry said as everyone was in silence not exactly sure what to say.

"Father God,

You are almighty. You are the reason we were even put here on this earth. We thank you Lord for givin' us the opportunity to know Mateo. To realize what a blessing he was to our sweet Livy. He became our family. Lord, we pray right now in this dark bunker that you help us to make it till the end. That you help us Lord to be strong until we see your face. Help us to see Mateo again one day. Not for our glory, but for yours. That we are doin' your business and that we make it to see you. There is evil in this world, and we pray that you help us to overcome that evil."

Livy had been too sick to realize what all had happened when Gin and Andy came back from losing Mateo. As she recovered from her fever over the following days, and was finally back to herself, she missed Mateo. He took a lot of time with her like a brother would. He would play ring toss with her with old canning rings, tic tac toe, he taught her how to climb a tree, and many times they would sit in the dirt and play with rolly pollies. He helped show her the beauty of nature.

Many times, he would talk to her about how God made things and why. "What do you think God was thinking when he made that bug?" Livy would laugh and he would tell her about some of the animals he had seen in the zoo. Livy had never been to a zoo but daydreamed about all the animals Mateo talked about.

He went out to get some supplies and found a simple children's book. It had a drawing of an elephant in it. "I also got you this!" he said excited to see her reaction and held out a small plastic elephant. She kept it in a special spot in the bunker where she kept everything Mateo brought her. She would take the book, and other things, out at night many times and look at what Mateo had brought back for her. She had special rocks that he would find and some dirty farm animals and dino-saurs that had once been left outside and buried in the dirt. She gave them a bath to try and clean them up, but they were weathered from being outside for who knows how many years.

She used her toothbrush to clean them, and her mom fussed at her for using her toothbrush. "Livy! We don't have another toothbrush! Why would you do this? Now I have to soak it in bleach, because you have to brush your teeth!" The family tried to make the most out of whatever they had and reuse certain items.

Livy didn't know anything different. She heard stories about grocery stores, hair salons, and something called going to the movies. The only time she saw a TV was when they were in Savy's house trying to get the thing to pick up a signal. She saw the news and couldn't imagine going to the movies to watch the news.

Chapter 16

She had blood running down her leg. They were dragging her along on the pavement. She was trying to get away, but their grip was tight, and they were not letting go. They were wearing masks and had guns. She didn't feel her gun on her back. They must've taken it when they tied her hands behind her back. The darkness had come in the middle of the day. It was like the sun started to dim and then it was dark. She tried to fight, but they hit her over the head with a gun. Now she realized she was being taken to a camp.

What if she had stayed with the guys she saw? Would she be going through all this now? She was nervous and scared about what was to come next. She could feel her face getting hot and pressure rising up in her chest. There was barbed wire around the whole compound. They took her into a separate fencing. The man with the mask looked at her sternly. She looked back into his eyes with a look of pleading sadness.

She looked around at where they had brought her and saw many gaunt faces. They were poor looking and fearful. On the other side of the compound there were lights shining like those on a football field and they could see people playing, but they all looked the same. They looked to be in uniform. Jules sat on the ground trying to gather her own thoughts and trying to figure out how on earth she was going to get out of all this mess. She needed to warn others what was to come. She had heard the news a couple of years ago talking about unity and everyone having the same things. That there would be happiness if you just listened. You wouldn't own anything, but you would be happy.

Certain things started to become very hard to get. Grocery stores were abandoned and going anywhere to scavenge became a danger. Jules and Savy had tried to become as self-reliant as they could. They had met certain farmers and people that were doing the same thing they were. Many people felt it was too little too late, but they had to keep on. Trying to live off the land was not easy, and many things had to be relearned. What was once common knowledge had become a distant memory.

A young woman sat down beside her. "This is the holding area." "Holding area for what," replied Jules. "Everyone that gets chipped and sanitized can go on the other side. They will get food. We have no choice. It is either listen or death." The woman kept glancing at the guards to make sure she was not being watched as she talked to Jules. "There are certain times each day when the loudspeaker sounds, and orders are given." Jules couldn't believe she was here. How was she going to get out? "I'm scared," the woman said. "I miss how my life was just a few years ago." "Me too," replied Jules. A man walked by talking to himself. "I can't...I can't...I can't go. I can't." He shook his head as he was walking.

Jules looked down at her torn bloody jeans. The slit in her leg was stinging. She was tired and her body ached. In silence she began to pray.

Lord Jesus Christ my mighty Savior, what shall I do next? I feel I'm about to die if they try and take me. I'm not sure why I am here or how I got into all this. Please help me. I'm in so much shock I don't even know what to pray. I just pray Lord that I see you in Heaven. Lord, I don't want to go to Hell. I pray all over for my salvation again. Lord, I just pray that I am your child. Help me. I'm scared to endure these things, but I also know that you will give me the strength needed. I love you, Lord.

She watched people on the other side. How it would be easy to just bend and take the chip, but the long-term side of that is living in eternal Hell. She remembered the many conversations she and Savy had about how it really sounded easier, but really, they are the ones enslaved. The people playing on the other side that get to eat. They are enslaved. *I can't let this happen,* thought Jules. Never had she thought 10 years ago that she would be living to see what she had seen already. She remembered sitting in church as a young girl hearing about The Great Tribulation, and how this was the wrath of God. God's wrath was not meant for His people, but to give another chance for the lost.

Jules went over to the young woman. "Listen," Jules said trying to get her attention. "You need to pray for the strength to stand strong for Christ. He is the one and only Savior. I'm going to try and get us out of here but know that we may die." The woman looked at Jules scared. Her hands were shaking. Jules grabbed her hands quickly. She glanced up at Jules with unbearable tears in her eyes. She could feel Jules' firm grasp on her hands.

"There is more than this. A lot more. We have to think of the bigger picture. Do you hear me?" She nodded and took a deep breath. "What is your name?" "Anna," answered the woman. "Anna, I'm Jules and it's okay to be scared. Sometimes we have to do things in the midst of fear. Now I'm going to sit back over here so the guards don't see us talking."

Jules looked outside the camp at the woods around them. *How did I get here,* she thought. As she sat there trying to think of a plan, she felt pain in her chest and the want in her. She knew she just wanted Jesus. The people in the camp were starving. They looked bony and tired.

Lord,

Let me not disappoint you. I know I have been Simon Peter at times, but in the end Lord he finished strong.

She felt the wind blow on her face. She felt chill bumps on her skin. The darkness made it hard to see, but there was a strange redness to the sky. Her hunger feeling was strong, and she saw the old man, eating dirt just to fill his stomach. There was a stench of feces and she kept swallowing, trying not to gag.

As she watched the guard, he caught her eye and started to move towards her. He started for her. She felt like she was going to vomit from nerves and the terrible smell. He took his gun and hit her on the jaw. She felt the blood running down her face. He grabbed her by the hair and pulled her head up while yelling at her in his language. Then spit on her calling her filthy. Jules laid there for hours. Anna trying to not even be seen just curled up with her head in her knees and her arms wrapped around her knobby legs.

Jules knew that she would probably die here. She worried about Savy and if she was okay. *I hope they hadn't already caught her. I pray Lord that she was strong if they did.* She felt swollen and couldn't move her jaw. She looked through the fence and saw the brush rustling. She kept watching trying to see what was beyond the brush, but it was hard to see.

She saw a flame that began to grow. She surveyed the woods but couldn't see anything. Just then she quickly glanced at the guards and heard alarms going off and they immediately tried to start putting out the fire that had now grown on the other side of the fence. Jules felt her heart pounding and looked over at Anna. "Anna," whispered Jules. Anna looked at Jules, then looked away.

Chapter 17

Savy realized that they were running out of food. They were eating very little, just enough to sustain themselves. Lou was weak and unable to stand. Lou's body needed electrolytes and she kept passing out. Savy gave her water from an old water bottle. She put table salt in the bottle and then carefully gave her that to help her have something in her body. If anyone should know about passing out it would be Savy. They were running out of rations yet were still trying everything they could. When they would go back up the other end of the tunnel that led to the house, they could hear people in there. They didn't dare make a sound.

Tucker went out to find anything he could for them. *He told me many times we have to focus on eternal life now, that this life is going to pass us by.* Savy was worried every time someone left the bunker. It had been amazing that no one had found them just yet. She wondered about Jules out there. Most people were captured or dead. The plants were starting to die from lack of sunlight and people were becoming more manic.

"Dear Lord,

Please be with Jules. Give her courage. If they have her Lord, help her escape. Give her boldness in Your mighty awesome name Lord Jesus. Have Your angels protect her very being. Guide her to where she needs to be. Send her Your angels to fight. Lord, You can speak and defeat Satan. I pray that they are defeated. She has always been there for me Lord and I pray that You are with her.

Savy didn't want to end the prayer. She prayed constantly for hours, as if an undeniable presence prompted her to pray hard for Jules.

Livy had been sleeping a lot here lately and her light seemed dimmed. Gin was busy emptying the five-gallon bucket that was used for restroom purposes. There was no difference in daytime and nighttime. It was all dark. It was all the same. Savy thought to herself how she missed the sun. She missed the way it felt on her skin. She tried to fill her head with memories and verses about what they were experiencing. She felt like she was going crazy. She remembered sweeping dust out of the tack room in the barn and the sunlight filtering the dust as it settled back down to the floor. The way her skin felt after swimming and laying out on a towel to dry out in the sun. Swatting flies off the horses in the sunset after a long ride. Memories of jumping into the lake and how the sunlight glistened off the ripples.

As she waited for Tucker to come back, she began feeling closed in. She had to step outside for just a little while. She needed to breathe fresh air. Tucker told her not to leave without him, but she was beginning to feel heavy in her chest and just needed to get out of the bunker. "Gin, I'll be back." "What, no you can't leave," she whispered. "I'll be fine. I just have to get some fresh air." "Savy, that's not a good idea. What if someone sees you." "Gin, watch the others, okay? I'm taking a bucket to get some more water." Gin gave her a look, not agreeing with her, but knew there was nothing she could do to stop her. How can someone stay inside this bunker forever and it's not like she's leaving for good.

She got to the other end of the tunnel and pushed out the door. She needed to feel the air. *Still dark,* thought Savy. She took a deep breath and looked around. She stepped out and ran behind a tree for cover. She had to walk a little way to gather some water and felt a rush to not get caught.

Livy had woken up and noticed that Savy wasn't there. Gin was busy with Lou. She was wiping her face off and talking to her. Livy snuck past them and went down the tunnel looking for Savy. She had her small plastic lamb in her hands gripping it tightly. The tunnel felt long and dark, Livy walked and then started to pick up the pace quickly as she started to feel icky from the dark tunnels. Halfway there she stopped and looked back towards the bunker and how dark it was but decided to keep going. She got to the ladder and began to climb up but heard voices. *Maybe that was Savy and Tucker,* Livy thought.

She pushed the door open and noticed hardwood floors and she stepped out quietly closing the door behind her. She was hidden in the closet and could see out of the cracks. A man in uniform had guns on him. He was looking over the table and talking to a woman. Livy noticed the man seemed mean. He would yell then walk over and slap the woman and then kiss her.

Livy was startled. She had never seen a man slap a woman. The woman was crying. Livy was scared, she had to get home. She took off running, her bare feet were pounding each board on the hardwood floor. The man turned when he heard her, he stopped with the woman, and started looking around. "Honey, I'm sorry. I'll be better. I'm sorry!" the woman cried. Livy began to pick up the pace even faster, darting towards the door. She grabbed the knob and turned it.

The man then stopped with the woman and began to walk out of the room. Livy could hear his boots getting closer. "Hey!" he yelled at Livy. She started outside, down the steps. She shouldn't have left the bunker. She was so scared and wanted her momma. She just ran as fast as she could. She didn't know how far he was behind her but had no time to look back. She felt he was close. She felt a tug on her tattered shirt, and he pulled her back.

Livy let out the biggest scream and was shaking with tears running down her face. Her hair was in her eyes, and she was kicking trying to get free. The man roughly moved her hair out of her face. He looked at her and smiled. "Did you sneak into my house last night for a place to stay?" he said looking at her. "Well, if I would've known you were there, we could've had some fun. I can take you to the fire tonight to get you all warm. You feel cold. Do you want to get warm?" Livy just grimaced at him as she squirmed.

Savy, running as fast as she could, knew that cry. *Livy must've left the bunker. I can't let anything happen to her. I'll never forgive myself.* Savy's heart was pounding, she knew she had to fight. She ran out to the edge of the woods and saw the man, and Livy struggling to get free. "Let her go," Savy said as she charged towards him.

He grabbed a knife and held it to Livy's neck. "You come any further and I will slit her throat." "I may want you little momma," as he looked at her with his evil intentions, laughing. "You tell me what I want to hear, and I'll let the little one go." Livy looked at Savy. "No!" cried Livy. "No don't." He tightened his grip on Livy. She could feel the cold blade against her neck.

"What!? Oh, what do you want from me? You can have me. Just let her go! Please!" screamed Savy frantically. She gasped for air as she was shaking, feeling sick inside. "Who is your Savior?" The man asked. "I want you to recant whoever you believe in and tell me who your Savior really is. You have seen him do miracles... no? You know who really heals. Tell me who you worship."

Livy squirmed and fought the cold blade against her neck, but the man's grip tightened around her. "Tell me now," yelled the man as he pressed harder. Savy was screaming and crying. Livy stiffened her neck with a deep breath, "you will bow before my Jesus one day. He is the only God," Livy said looking at Savy intently. The man started to cut her throat but fell to his knees as Tucker ran up behind them with his bow and grabbed Livy. "I...I'm... There's a..." "Shhh," replied Tucker, hugging Livy. "Don't speak." Savy ran up to Livy and cradled her. The arrow went through the soldier's left shoulder into his heart. Tucker pulled the arrow out and they headed back to the bunker.

Gin frantically met them halfway back to the bunker, where all the commotion happened, as she was trying to find Livy. "Oh no! No," she said feeling like she couldn't get to her fast enough. She met Savy, who was carrying Livy, and fell to her knees. "Put pressure on her neck." Savy felt the guilt that she had even left the bunker. "I'm getting water to clean her." Gin held her fingers to the slit on her throat and kissed her head all over. "Oh, Livy! Livy...Livy. You're my girl, Livy. Please God don't take her from me! I can't go on without her. Please God."

Tucker picked Livy up, holding her wound firmly, and carried her through the tunnel as Gin followed. Ms. Lou opened the door and was pacing the floor. "My heavens. Oh, what happened to my girl? We have to be more careful. Lord, you see this. You know what's going on. You know what she needs Lord. Heal her. Lord!" "Savy!" Tucker said, "We need bandages and antibiotic ointment. Savy went to the pantry and shuffled through everything to try and find what Livy needed. She pulled out the first aid kit, and handed it over to Gin, and began to fan Livy. Gin poured straight alcohol on her wound and tried to thread the needle, but her hands were too shaky. Tucker pacing the floor bent down and steadied her hands. She gave him the needle. He managed to get three stitches in. Livy slept for hours while Gin watched her chest rise and fall all night.

Savy slid her back down the dirt wall full of complete exhaustion. Tucker sat in front of her. Her eyes were swollen from crying. He lifted her chin up. "I love you, Savy." She frowned and felt immense grief. *I can't breathe.* She started gasping and breathing heavy. "Look in my eyes," Tucker said holding her face and steadying her. "Breathe in. Now breathe out. Slowly. Think and listen to your breathing. Hear me?" She nodded and slowed her breathing. She fell asleep on his shoulder, and he gently picked her up and carried her to bed.

Chapter 18

Henry, Andy, and Leroy came in from hunting. They were not greeted, but instead saw the exhaustion in the room. They pulled a few squirrels out of their cloth bags. Tucker reached for his jacket and covered Savy as she slept. Ms. Lou came over and started skinning one of the squirrels. Henry grabbed her hand, "Manna Lou sit down." "I can't, everyone has had a rough day," she answered back. "You are just now gettin' very little strength back and you shouldn't worry yourself with this right now." Lou looked at Henry, "How can I sit and do nothing? This is the least I can do." "But today I'm tellin' you to sit and sin' to that sweet Livy." "Livy went out the tunnel without telling anyone," her eyes filled with tears. "It was my fault, I was weak, and Gin was worrying with me and trying to help me get my strength back," Ms. Lou said, wringing her hands. "Manna Lou, there is so much goin' on right now we can't blame anyone for what we are experiencin' right now. An evil, like we have never known, is rampant. Andy and I saw an evil today that we had never seen. We can't keep evil from any of us, because it's out there. We have to make sure that we are very careful."

"What happened Henry? Are you okay?" "Manna Lou, I hate to even tell you, but I know that you may see thin's anyway." "Henry, I wasn't born yesterday, and I've heard some pretty bad things in my lifetime." He looked down at the dirt floor and raised his eyes up at her, filled with water like a dam that was about to break. He tried holding back the tears, but they were about to flow down like a waterfall. "Oh Manna Lou, it's just so bad. I have such a hard time sayin' what was goin' on. It's beyond evil. My heart can't fathom all of it, and what if we aren't untouched." Ms. Lou took her old wrinkly hands and cupped Henry's bearded face. She kissed his cheek and looked deep into his eyes. He saw her love and kindness and he couldn't imagine not having the people he loved dearly around him during this time.

"Oh, to just be able to give up. Have you ever thought about just taking the mark Henry?" "No ma'am. You can't either. That is a fleetin' time of gettin' it a little easier, but this ma'am, is different. Every time you think about givin' up, I want you to think of burnin' in Hell forever. Your skin is bein' charred up, your body is continually dyin' and there is nothin' you can do." "Well, Henry, that is what we have to stick to. You can't give up and neither will I. He has given us love and this makes us see evil."

What is it that you saw," Ms. Lou pressed again. "There was a fire and people were sacrificin' others over it. There was a dark laughter, and I didn't stick around too long. When Andy and I saw it, we got outta there. I felt as though my heart was poundin' and I couldn't leave fast enough." Ms. Lou grabbed his hand, "And do not fear those who kill the body but cannot kill the soul. But rather fear Him who is able to destroy both soul and body in Hell." Wiping his eyes with one hand he pulled Ms. Lou close with the other and hugged her tightly. He began weeping more and managed to get a word out.

"You've been readin'," he spoke. "I have nothing else to get me through this, but He will. If they take our lives Henry, they cannot take our souls." "Oh, Manna Lou, you sure know how to put us in the right perspective and in our place." "That's not me honey. That's Jesus our Lord doing that. Now give me that knife and let me take care of these squirrels. I think everybody has missed you today." As Ms. Lou continued skinning the squirrels she thought, *this is a punishment for the unbelievers and for the people who had chances to accept and would not accept Him. We have this last chance to follow, and I have to get this right. This is a time to believe Jesus now and stand strong. If we continue in faith now, we will not have eternal punishment.*

Andy kissed Livy on the head and squeezed Gin's hand tightly. "I should've known she had left. I should've stopped her, but I didn't know." "We can all say that Gin. I should've been here to protect you and Livy, but I wasn't. What does that say about me? I have never seen a darkness in people the way Henry and I saw it when we were out." Gin wrapped her arms around Andy. "How can we go on like this?" "That's just it, I don't know. I wish I had all the right words, but I don't."

Livy gasped. They all gathered around her, and she peeked her eyes open. She looked pale from losing blood, but she was still breathing. "Andy," Livy managed to get out hoarsely. "Yes, baby?" Andy rubbed her arm and grabbed on to her hand. "We can't give up His name. We can't bow to these evil people. God showed me that we have a place." "What is this place like Livy?" "The houses are made of wood, but grown that way just for us. It's colorful but hard to explain. There are angels that seem to be very big with many faces."

Henry listened and went and grabbed his Bible. He opened it up to Ezekiel 1:5-11 (NKJV). He began to read to the group.

> Also, from within it *came* the likeness of four living creatures. And this *was* their appearance: they had the likeness of a man. Each one had four faces, and each one had four wings. Their legs *were* straight, and the soles of their feet *were* like the soles of calves' feet. They sparkled like the color of burnished bronze. The hands of a man *were* under their wings on their four sides; and each of the four had faces and wings. Their wings touched one another. *The creatures* did not turn when they went, but each one went straight forward. As for the likeness of their faces, *each* had the face of a man; each of the four had the face of a lion on the right side, each of the four had a face of an ox on the left side, and each of the four had the face of an eagle. Thus *were* their faces. Their wings stretched up-

> ward; two *wings* of each one touched one another, and two covered their bodies.

"Livy does this sound like what you saw?" Andy asked. Everyone listened intently. You could've heard a pin drop. "I can see those faces and it was like something I've never seen before. A creature that was big and strong. God's angels." They all stared in amazement. They needed to hear encouragement and they all felt His Spirit in that little bunker at that exact moment.

They all began laying hands on Livy and asking for the Holy Spirit to heal Livy's wound. They prayed that she would get her strength back. They took this time to fall on their knees and really pray like warriors around her bed. They had learned to lean on God and lean on each other. There was a closeness between them all in the bunker. A family. After hearing encouragement from God out of the mouth of a child, this was the first night in a long time that they all got rest. They had all grown weary and sick from lack of food and water, lack of sunlight, and lack of fresh air. However, tonight God knew just what they needed, and they felt Him there at that moment. He gave them food even in the midst of all the chaos of the day. They ate squirrel to have something in their stomachs.

Henry couldn't help but feel that this was meant for them to hear from Livy. He had tried to be so strong for everyone else and just move on to the next thing they needed for survival. He too realized he needed rest. *I've seen his beautiful creation here and I'm sure what's going on here is unfathomable in Heaven.* Henry slowly drifted off as he thought about a praise song he would hear Maggie sing.

He is Lord, He is Lord.

He has risen from the dead, and He is Lord.

Every knee shall bow, every tongue confess, that Jesus Christ is Lord.

Chapter 19

Landon and Tate found a long narrow ditch away from the camp. They inched their way down into the ditch that had roots sticking out in various areas of the dirt. They could hear the alarms that were going off from the fire.

She's going to try, Landon said to himself as sweat poured down his face, *she's got to.* Tate looked over at Landon and could see the uncertainty in his face. "Look Landon, we can't get captured ourselves." "We can't just leave her there either." Tate wanting to help...but realizing they barely knew this girl...was caught between two thoughts. "She obviously can hold her own," replied Tate. "No, no, you know what they will do to her. They will kill her Tate," pleaded Landon. "Or, worse," Tate contested.

Landon put his boot in one of the roots and began to climb up out of the ditch. Tate grabbed his arm. "Wait, Landon, you can't just go in there acting like Superman or something." Landon pulled his arm back with a little bit of disgust on his face. "No, but I know I can't just sit here and listen or think what if we would've tried either." He pulled himself out and crawled back towards the camp. Dreading the outcome of it all, Tate followed Landon.

Landon and Tate heard soldiers and saw the glaze against the sky from the bright lights, but it wasn't until Landon realized what had happened to Jules that he decided they needed to do something. He watched her for a few hours, trying to develop a plan to help her escape. One that hopefully didn't involve them becoming captured. He kept waiting to see if she would even look in his direction. Suddenly, she did. Almost like she had given up hope. Like she was staring off into the unknown. Like she had nothing left to give. As Landon squatted wondering what her exact thoughts were, he began lighting the brush in the woods. The sparks soon took to more bushes until it formed a line on one side of the whole compound. The guards started running towards Tate and Landon, though not seeing them.

Looking back at the camp the guards could see Jules almost over the gate. The guard standing watch in the tower fell from the tower after being shot. His body hit the ground. One of the guards was almost back to the compound when she jumped down on the other side of the gate and took off running full force trying to get to the woods. Landon slung his gun over his back and watched to see if she would win the race against her life, realizing it was not working in her favor. Tate started yelling and running to distract their attention onto him. Landon felt a pit in his stomach and didn't know what to do but run. He ran in the woods towards the direction Jules was running. He was running after her. Jules, not realizing who was behind her for the longest time, just continued to run. She felt as if her lungs were filled with cold air. The darkness made it that much harder, but she couldn't stop. They were still after her. Until she tripped and Landon caught up to her.

Both panting for air she looked at him putting her hands on her knees breathing in as if she had been playing a game of baseball. As their breathing slowed Landon heard a gunshot and heard Tate scream. He fell to his knees putting his hands behind his neck and wailed out a cry that Jules had never heard before. He hit his hands to the bare ground and dug his fingers into the dirt and grass. He felt as if he'd been punched in the stomach hard and lost all breath. Jules bent on her knees and covered his back with her arm almost to cradle him. She had no words, but she knew that the other guy that was with him before was no longer there. He couldn't say much of anything, but she grabbed his hands. "We have to go now." They got up trying not to attract attention in their direction, not really knowing what direction to go, but they knew they had to get as far away from the camp as possible.

They found an old barn halfway standing and decided to try and find a place to lay. Their bodies were sore. Landon noticed her shirt torn above her hip. "Your shirt," Landon pointed. Jules looked down and felt her torn shirt. Opening the slit, she then jerked her hand back. "Ahhh," she looked at her hands and noticed blood. Landon took his shirt off and tore it in two, making a bandage to wrap around her waist.

"I think I'm okay," she said still hurting from the sting of her hand touching it. "Just let me help," Landon replied. "I think you have helped me..." she trailed off realizing she hadn't even gotten his name. "Landon." "Landon," Jules repeated in a whisper as she smirked her mouth to one side, unsure if she should even smile. "I'm Jules. Thank you for saving my life back there," she said in a nervous tone. "Tate saved your life," Landon corrected her.

"What happened...You know what, you don't even have to tell me." She sat down on the cold hard dirt. "I waited and watched you for hours in that compound trying to think about how I would even get you out. I didn't even know if you would try. So, I waited and watched you and when you were sitting there looking like you had lost hope, I started the fire."

"How did you know that I was captured?" "I didn't. We heard soldiers and saw the brightness of the lights." Landon said as he looked down tracing the dirt. Jules shared, "The lights were shining on these people of all ages. They got food and clothes. They took the mark." "They took the mark?" Landon questioned her looking up. "They had to recant their God and believe in who they wanted you to believe in. Savy says this is the Antichrist. Someone who really isn't God but acts as if he is. Even performing miracles." "I remember hearing about this from some of my family. I didn't really understand it all." "Scripture says that if you take this mark you will burn in eternity."

"So, you think these people were raptured?" Landon asked. "I don't think, I know the Lord took them," Jules said with a passion in her voice. "This is not all there is." "Well, some have talked of aliens and I'm not saying I believe that. There have just been a lot of unexplainable things going on, and honestly sometimes I don't know what to believe."

"I get it, but there isn't a lot of time left." "Everyone that left me were believers, so I believe it was more than aliens. Although, people have mentioned seeing them and weird objects in the sky, and they move like no technology we've ever had." "I think these aliens that people are seeing are not aliens. I think they are demonic. I think Satan is smart and he is trying to do anything he can to keep people from believing. He doesn't have much time left either. The spiritual world is real, and they are working overtime," Jules said. She was surer of herself than she'd ever been. "My wife was like you." "How so?" Jules asked. "Passionate." "I wasn't always passionate, but when everyone vanished…and they were all believers in Jesus…I had to think about it. I made so many stupid mistakes in my life. I can't and won't get this one wrong."

"I wanted to help and get you out, but I froze when everything happened. I wanted to be there for you. Tate did that so the soldiers would be distracted. I know he did," Landon said leaning his head back against the old barnwood. His eyes were swollen. Jules touched the side of his face and leaned over kissing his cheek. "And nothing I will ever say will ever help or show how grateful I am for y'all."

Landon turned his head as her hands went down his neck feeling his shoulder muscle. He rubbed down the side of her arm. She sat over him and began kissing him rubbing her hands through his hair and feeling herself brush against his hard chest. Her body felt more alive than it had in years. As his hands began to wander she stopped them. "Landon." "Yes," he whispered breathing heavy. "I can't," she said, as she shifted onto the ground beside him.

He put his arm around her, and she fell asleep on his chest.

Chapter 20

Everyone was moving slowly as they all began to wake up. Lou had made some dandelion tea for Livy to sip on. Gin was asleep on the floor next to Livy. She had one hand on Livy and stayed awake all night watching her daughter's chest rise and fall. "Our God is powerful and Livy, He listened to us last night." Livy gave Lou a smirk, and wiggled up to sit, resting her head against the dirt wall. "You are my baby too. I enjoy watching you grow," Ms. Lou said holding out her tea to Livy. "Livy tell me more about your dream."

Livy's eyes widened and she looked as though her pale face had melted off and a new brightness glowed within her face.

"Manna, it was beautiful. The mansion we all lived in had many rooms. Andy was there and we walked out the back door and there were big green fields. There was a garden with statues of lions and water was flowing out of their mouths. As we walked out of the garden, we started walking down a hill and there was a wedding going on. The bride was beautiful. It felt sunny and I had the best feeling in my body. It's hard to describe but everything seemed perfect." Ms. Lou smiled at Livy and put her arm around her.

"You can't leave us and go walking off. What would I do if I didn't have you? Who would take care of me?" Lou said chuckling, but also knew it was embedded with truth. "I won't ever again. I promise. The man was scary Manna, but God is bigger." "It's true Livy, God is so much bigger." She patted her leg, "You know, your mom has been through a lot, and she is one tough cookie." Livy looked at her mom lying on the floor, and she leaned up and brushed the hair away from her face. "I love you," Livy whispered.

Andy and Tucker had their guns on their backs as they walked for miles and miles to find anything that would be of use. They really wanted to find more medicine, but most of the medicines had been ransacked. They tried to avoid areas where they had seen so much evil. They had all grown so tired and hungry, their bodies were becoming weak, and they felt so depressed. It was still dark. The darkness made it hard for them, but they had to continue.

Tucker thought about the feeling of the warm sun. He thought about the animals that he had taken care of for Savy's parents. How he wished that he could go back to those days, just being on the farm and feeding them. He would make sure that all were accounted for and that they were all in good shape. Many times, he would have to check on the market lambs to make sure they were not prolapsing. He would also take care of the flock and castrate and dock all the sheep. He remembered the first time he had to do these procedures. He was a little disgusted, but didn't show it because he didn't want to be perceived as a wuss.

After that he realized that was the first of many gross things on the farm that he would experience. From engorged udders, newborns, and bad wounds that became abscessed too quickly. These became second nature after he had been doing it over the years. Tucker thought to himself, *I guess I became a little used to farm life and found myself not getting attached to the animals as much. I came to know it was just farm life and animals would die eventually. I remembered tearing up when my favorite breeding ewe had passed away and Savy's dad, without acting like he saw me tearing up said, "You know Tucker, God gave man dominion over the fish of the sea, the birds of the air, over the cattle, the wild animals, and anything that creeps on the earth." I remembered him saying that with such a peace. "This is why we do this. Farming is hard work. I've had my fair share of questions when it comes to animals, and they are smarter than we give them credit for, but they are animals." He finished cleaning out the horse stall and let me think on his words.*

"Should we keep going?" Andy whispered as he stumbled upon voices. Tucker got down and tried to peak over the old rusted out car beside what they thought was an empty house. There were women being held at gunpoint and being made to remove their clothes. Tucker and Andy saw that the women were scared and were shaking. Their ribs were showing, and they looked as if they hadn't eaten in days. Their hair was frizzy and looked disheveled.

"No! Please!" one woman said as she was shaking with her arms folded around her stomach as if she was hugging herself. The man slapped her and grabbed both of her arms moving closer to her as if he was getting some sort of satisfaction out of it. Andy began to quietly get his gun ready. The man threw her on the ground and began taking her clothes off. She squirmed and tried to fight him.

Tucker motioned to Andy to go ahead, and Andy then aimed and took a shot at the man that was in the process of unzipping his pants. Right as the commotion started with the women screaming, Tucker had his sight on the second man, who was looking around as he held the other woman down. As the second man fell to the ground, the two women franticly began scrounging for their clothes. Andy and Tucker gave them a minute and when they felt the women were dressed, they kept their guns in their arms and slowly walked up. There was a little girl only in underwear. She was dirty and looked to need a bath. She looked about Livy's age and Andy couldn't stand to see her in this condition. What if that had been Livy?

The women invited Andy and Tucker into the house. "We don't need to come in, ma'am. We just wanted to be of help to you." "Please don't leave us. We have nowhere to go and with the gunshots others will come. I'm sure they heard."

"Who heard?" Andy said. "There are more coming," they said in fear. "We may have things you need." Andy and Tucker looked at each other, knowing they were in need. These women and little girl looked pitiful. Andy pulled Tucker aside. "We can't leave them," Andy whispered. Tucker looked at the men lying there on the ground. "We don't have enough supplies to care for them." "Are we to worry about this earthly body? What would our Jesus want us to do?"

When Andy put it like that Tucker knew he was right, placing his hands on the back of his head and grasping his hair, sighing, he gave up. He gave up himself. He knew that they were to only think of others and not themselves. He knew that what they did here on earth mattered. He remembered reading about the prayers of the saints in Revelation. "Okay," Tucker said with another sigh, not knowing how this would affect the others at the bunker.

"Why don't you come with us, and we can get you some water and whatever else we can find." The lady, with her leathery looking face, had a tear run down her cheek. "You would do this for us?" "We are called to be like Jesus. That's the only way to truly survive." Without fully understanding what he meant, the woman grabbed her daughter up and kissed her cheek. She whispered, "I'm so sorry," in her ear. The little girl wrapped her arms around her neck. "Do you mind if we look around the house to see if there is anything that might be of any use to us?" Tucker said. He knew supplies were diminishing. "Not at all, we will need to grab some things anyway."

They walked upon the old boards, which had cracks in them, and it was easy to see the dirt falling in between the cracks. It was obvious that once upon a time this house used to be very nice, but the world had taken its toll on it. "Just look around and take whatever you need." Andy went into the bathroom and started to look in the cabinets and behind the mirror. There were old bottles of prescriptions. Without really knowing what was what, Andy grabbed a pillowcase and dumped all the medicine in there. The lady grabbed an old bottle of homemade wine that was probably more like moonshine now and handed it to Tucker. He put it in his backpack, and they grabbed a few blankets. Andy saw the little girl's room. She didn't have much, but a few toys. The little girl was holding a little baby doll that had one eye stuck. She was holding her like a real baby. She saw that Andy was putting stuff in a pillowcase and the little girl put some things in there too, including her baby doll. She smiled at Andy, and he smiled back.

Chapter 21

"Anna!" Jules said as her face was appearing out of the darkness. She kept looking at the gate. Then looking back to the woods. Then up at the barbed wire where it hit the sky. Anna's face kept popping up right in front of hers and she was crying. She was crying and screaming. Anna was skin and bones and she was looking at her with that gaunt face. Her eyes had dark circles and her skin was pale. Her hair was stringy, long, and black. Jules had a feeling of urgency and panted really hard. She felt sweaty and kept looking back behind her. She could see some people playing and happy, but Anna wasn't. It was daylight but the clouds were coming and covering them all. She felt the darkness. It was thick and hot. "Anna!"

"Anna!" Jules woke up screaming, sitting straight up again. Landon grabbed her quickly. "Shhhh. Hey. Hey. Jules. It's okay. You're here with me. It's okay. What happened?" "She was in my head. She is scared. That's why she screamed at the....at the guard. She is just scared." Jules said, wiping her tears out of her eyes. Her voice sounding raspy still trying to fully wake up. "She ratted me out. I told her to stand strong and to not take the mark. I told her, but she's just so scared. She wouldn't follow me." Landon just hugged Jules and held her close. They could hear the crickets and felt sore from laying on the bare ground.

Landon sat there trying to console Jules, "I have bad dreams too." "What kind of bad dreams?" "They haunt me at night a lot," Landon said sighing. "I see my family leaving me. Floating up. As if they are just leaving me and I feel as if I have this gaping hole. I feel that every day. Like something is missing. They are missing."

Jules sat up and was rubbing her eyes, like a little girl trying to wake up. She felt hot and pinched her shirt moving it away from her body trying to fan herself. "Landon, that something missing hurts. I know, but Jesus is the big something that is missing. He is the only one who can save, the only one that can truly fill that emptiness." "It's hard to feel anything right now." "I know," responded Jules. "But He is here. It's not always easy to feel Him. Sometimes we have to work at it. We have to make that relationship grow and I believe when He sees that we are serious, He will work in our lives."

She paused, waiting for a response. "It's like with your family. If you didn't try with them and you just expected them to always do what you wanted them to do without having a relationship with them, and without talking to them, how can they really feel loved in return. Does that make sense?"

"Yeah, I just have a hard time knowing what to say." "I say, you have to start somewhere, but just know He is mighty.

He deserves reverence. He isn't a genie in a bottle. He is Lord of all creation. He is just with righteousness. Humble yourself before Him. I think our world seemed to go away from that at one time. Remember how some churches started to have a stage, a coffee bar, lights, and a pastor that seemed untouchable. We forget that we weren't the ones to be catered to. We are the ones that need to be ready to serve. We left the churches that were small in numbers, but big in their faith. Now I'm not saying that all bigger churches are bad, but things seemed to get blurry. Like people forgot the importance of true fellowship. We have to be okay without all the stuff. We needed to give and receive the Gospel in a raw, humble, and true way. Just true obedience."

"I would only go to church on Easter and Christmas or if there was something special the kids were doing. I should've listened more," he said looking up. "We all should've listened more." "Does that make sense though? Church became something different than what God would've wanted, I think. It became a social event. A business. It became somewhat selfish."

"So how did it happen for you? The 'Big Change?'" Jules asked Landon. "My son and I were at a football game together. Tate and his boy were with us too. Tate and I have been friends for a long time. We were in the Marines together and volunteered every year at the football games. Tate went to get drinks at the concession stand and I stayed with the boys. One minute we were cheering in the stands and the next minute they were gone. Vanished. Their clothes were there, but they weren't. I've replayed it in my head about a million times." "What happened to Tate?" "It took a while to find him, and everyone was just more frantic than I had ever seen. When I got to him, he wouldn't leave until he saw the clothes. He held his son's jersey for days. Like he was just going to reappear, but we were made to leave when people started getting violent." "It's crazy the different stories I've heard," Jules said, leaning on her arm with her hair draping over. "Where were you?" Landon asked.

"I was part of a team of stylists in New York. I was asked to go to Boston, Massachusetts for a big hair show. Beforehand the stylists gathered in a salon close to the convention. We were finishing up prepping our example customers for the day." She wrapped her hair behind her ear and moved her knees up to her chest. Landon listened intently. "I was curling a lady's hair for the special event, and she was just gone. I can't really explain it, but I dropped my curling iron. I began to feel dizzy. I started looking around and my good friend that was working beside me was gone as well. Her hair dryer was laying on the ground still going. Another lady was sitting in the chair screaming. I didn't know what to say and I reached for my phone. I could hear people in the streets outside our building. It sounded chaotic, and I was scared to go anywhere. I locked the door and called my sister, Kim. There was no answer. I started dialing other family members and Savy. Finally, she answered after I had been calling for about an hour. We didn't really know what to do and we were both in shock.

I didn't know how to help the lady that was so upset. She looked so afraid. I grabbed her hands and gently told her that she was more than welcome to stay with me if she couldn't get anyone. Her husband did eventually come and get her. We turned on the news as we waited for him. He had trouble even getting to her. She threw herself into a bit of a panic attack worried that her husband wouldn't come. I gave her a bag to breathe in and I just kept telling her to breathe slowly. I remember feeling inside that I wasn't holding it together myself either. The next morning, I packed up and checked out of the hotel. I ended up driving to Savy's back in New York City. She has been my best friend since school, and we grew up together. It took me days to get home from all the wreckage and debris." "I never thought we would see anything like this. It always seemed so out of touch with reality when people would talk about the rapture. But here we are."

"We need to be finding water. Maybe if we were to follow the creek bed it will lead us to Savy," Jules said thinking of the best way to get to her. They ended up not going back to sleep. Both were awake at this point. Landon dusted himself off and held out his hand to Jules. She looked up at him and grabbed his hand. She pulled herself up and her body was facing his. He felt her side and moved his hand down the side of her hip. Her face was against his and she felt the warmth of his skin. She felt a feeling of excitement all over her body.

Then all of the sudden they heard this unusual sound and a scraping on the tin roof of the barn. It sounded dark and Jules wrapped her arms in fear around Landon. He had one arm around her tightly and grabbed his lighter with the other. This sound was of darkness and something they had never heard before. She could feel the evil in this moment, and it tried to come for Landon. It showed its face to Landon, but Jules had both arms wrapped around his torso and had her face buried in his chest.

She was praying loudly against this evil. "Lord! Jesus! You are more powerful than this evil. Flee from us. I am the Lord's! My Lord Jesus Christ will protect me from all evil! I cry out for help! Jesus! Jesus!" Things then became really quiet, as if a pin could drop. Jules looked up at Landon and he was still frozen in a blank stare. She reached up to his face. He looked down at her. Feeling as if he could barely breathe, he fell to his knees. "I don't know..." Landon stammered. "I don't know where to start to accept Him, but I know I have to." He said he was more nervous than he had ever been. Jules bent down with him and right there in the quietness, with their knees on the dirty barn floor, they began to pray and in that moment they had a brightness radiate all around them. Landon looked up and felt his breathing change. He knew he had been saved, and that the demon that came couldn't get him now.

They prayed over their journey, and they walked for a while, eventually making it onto an old school bus. The weeds had grown and taken over the bus, covering the windows. Just as they had gotten in it, it started to rain. Jules sat down in one of the seats and Landon sat beside her. She rested her head on his shoulder, grabbed his hand, and began to recite the Lord's prayer. "Our Father who art in Heaven, hallowed be Thy name. Your kingdom come. Your will be done on earth as it is in Heaven. Give us this day our daily bread. And forgive us our trespasses as we forgive those who trespass against us. Lead us not into temptation, but deliver us from evil. For Thine is the Kingdom and the Glory for ever and ever. Amen." "Amen." Landon held her hand and rubbed her thumb with his. He kissed her forehead, and they drifted off to sleep from the total exhaustion of the day.

Chapter 22

Gin and Savy had water in a five-gallon bucket and were helping the two women wash off. Their hair had been matted and they were able to put it in a braid. "What is your name? Gin asked. "Hanna," she replied. She looked tired. Gin dipped the rag into the water and washed her back. As the water flowed out of the rag down her back, she saw a scar on her back but didn't ask any questions.

"Are you okay?" Gin asked. "I am, but I don't know about my Sissy girl." She looked over at her. Her little girl was playing with Livy. Livy was thrilled to see another child. She had never seen another little person. She hardly knew how to play because she was very mature, but she was excited to see her. She took her by the hand, but the other girl snatched her hand away not knowing what to think. Then Livy gave her one of the only toys she owned, one of her little plastic animals. Livy laid her head over on the lazy basset hound, and smiled back at Sissy. "Why are her toes pink?" Sissy said, squatting down pointing to Susy's paws. Livy laughed, "My Mateo brought me back fingernail paint. My momma painted my nails, and I decided to paint Susy's!" Sissy laughed and looked at Leroy's toes to see if his were also painted. "He doesn't sit still enough for me to paint," Livy said explaining, "and he is a boy." Sissy smiled and realized that Livy just wanted a friend. Hanna didn't want her little girl out of her sight, especially after everything they had been through.

"That girl knows about rocking that baby doll." The other lady spoke up, "All she does is rock her baby." "She must have learned that from her momma," Savy spoke up. "She has a natural mother's instinct," the woman replied. "What is your name?" asked Savy. "I'm Kyra, and this is Hanna. We have been friends for most of our lives. Never thought we would have gone through this terrible hell that we've been through."

"Where were ya'll when the 'Big Change' happened?" Kyra had dark skin with braids tight to her head. She seemed so down to earth like she would talk to anybody. *When I asked her that question, her eyes became sad.* She didn't cry, but instead tried to hold back any tears that she felt were trying to come. She paused before answering, "I...I'm sorry Kyra, I didn't mean to trigger any upset feelings." "Honey, no you're fine. You're fine. Just gathering my thoughts is all. I'm okay."

"My husband Miles was on a flight home. He never came home. We had two children that left. I was at the playground that day. I told both my boys that I would take them that day. Their daddy was going to be home that night. The park we go to has a walking track all the way around it, and it goes over a bridge where a creek flows. Now Hanna was pregnant at the time. Her feet were actually swollen that day and she decided to rest at home. Only she ended up getting a phone call and having to go show a house."

She put her hands up to her face and slowly took a breath. "I'm sorry. I feel like not a day goes by that I don't see their faces. It's like they're in my dreams. Do you think God gives us dreams of our family?" "I do actually," Savy responded. "Whether they are simply for comfort or to show us something, I do." She had her eyes closed for a moment as she spoke and put her palms facing out almost as if she was praising Jesus. "They were saying, chase me momma. Chase me! They were laughing. I remember the breeze that day. I remember laughing."

"My laughter turned into screaming and crying. You see I didn't know what had just happened. I didn't realize God...," she put her hand up to her mouth as it was hard for her, "...God was actually saving my sons. They were innocent. I can't explain a lot, but I remember listening to my family. You see we grew up in Mobile, Alabama. They were God fearing people, my family. Me, on the other hand, I didn't fear Him enough. Oh, how I regret my decision. He has left me, and He has forgotten me. We have been through so much. There is nowhere to go. Savy, it is evil out there."

"I know Kyra. It is pure evil, but God has not forgotten you. You were lost, but we still have a chance to make things right." "You think we do?" Kyra looked with distress on her face. "I do." As they all began to share stories, they learned Hanna's story as well.

Hanna had been at work in Nashville. She was a realtor and went to meet a couple she had been working with for the past month. They had called and were so excited about a house, they were ready to put an offer on it. People were moving to Tennessee by the thousands from all over and were calling it the mass exodus from California. She was a very successful realtor, who kept up with all her clients.

They were standing in the great room of this beautiful house.

The house was a two-story old southern house with navy shutters. The front porch looked like a Southern Living Magazine with a big beautiful wooden swing that hung on the porch by a rope. As they went over the contract, his wife disappeared. Just gone. She said she had never seen a man so distraught. He got down looking through her clothes and found her wedding band. As the man and Hanna walked outside together, they immediately saw chaos. The man ended up helping Hanna get back to the countryside.

Gin had a speck of happiness in her heart that Livy would have someone to play with, talk to, and just be with. Everyone was in for at least the next eight hours. Even though there had not been any sunlight or electricity for a long time, they tried to keep track of the daytime hours versus what would be the actual nighttime hours. For now, just for a small fraction of time, they felt like their family had grown.

Maybe it was a blessing from God. Maybe it was because He knew what everyone was going through and how everyone needed like-minded people. Most people during this time, like Gin, Savy, and the rest, knew they had to reach out and help. *This is what God calls us to do.* Romans 15:1 (NKJV) says, We then who are strong ought to bear with the scruples of the weak, and not to please ourselves.

Most were trying to make it on their own. They were fearful and kept food all for themselves, *but we know that God takes care of even the birds of the air. If we do what is right, he will be with us and provide.* Proverbs 19:17 (NKJV) says He who has pity on the poor lends to the LORD, And He will pay back what He has given. *Each of us have been growing paler and dark under our eyes.*

Andy and Tucker made some beans, and that along with love and kindness, was what God knew was needed. *We had grown tired of the same food, but this was better than what some had. All we needed was to have something in our bellies before sleep.* Gin many times wondered and imagined what happened to Bret.

Did he take the mark or come to his senses that this was all about control? She knew she would probably never know, but she prayed for him daily. He was Livy's dad and that was the least she could do. Maybe once she's there in Heaven, she will see his face. She had a love for him because he was the father of her sweet child, but she had to move on from him. Grateful she did and God had other plans to give her Andy. Andy goes above and beyond to make sure we are comfortable. He loves Livy like she is his own. That kind of love is from Jesus. It is sacrificial.

Chapter 23

Jules gasped awake and felt hot and sweaty. She had to go use the bathroom. "Landon, I'm stepping outside. I have to use the bathroom." "I'm going with you." "No, you're not," Jules replied, thinking he was crazy. "Listen, who cares if you have to pee? Everyone does it, but I don't want you to be alone. What if someone, or something like that demonic thing we saw, is out there?" "Oh, whatever. Just turn around. Okay?" "You got it," Landon said rolling his eyes at her.

She pulled her pants up. "Okay, you can turn back around," she said chuckling as she was zipping her pants. "Are you wanting to keep walking or rest more." "I think I'm up now; I can't seem to turn my mind off. I had another strange nightmare. I couldn't get to Savy." "You'll have that. It's like you live in the nightmare, sleep in the nightmare, and then wake up to a nightmare." "I heard helicopters all night last night and I couldn't sleep much myself," Landon said, as he was hiding himself behind the bus taking his turn. Maybe we should find some water. Jules lifted her arm and smelled her own body odor, "I can't be smelling good." Landon smiled, "I could say the same." She really hadn't noticed if he smelled bad because she was worried enough about her own smell. "How is your side?" Landon asked pointing to their makeshift bandage. "It's okay, I guess. Just sore."

They started quietly walking to find water. It seemed like they walked a long way before finding a creek. When they did, they followed it until it was deep enough to bathe off in. "You go first. I'm going to keep watch while you're in there." Landon turned and leaned on a tree trying not to look but felt himself glancing in her direction more than once. She left her clothes next to him and he could see her silhouette. Her outline was beautiful as she got into the water.

She dunked her hair in, feeling the cold water rush over her. Cold but feeling refreshed, as it had been too long since she had washed up. *I can't believe that the man who died for me...I held at gunpoint,* she pondered as she was gathering her thoughts. It had all been a lot to take in. *Poor Landon. He must've thought a lot of Tate. He must think a lot of me, but for what? I wouldn't say we had a good introduction, that's for sure.* All these thoughts swirled in her mind. She got out squeezing out her hair and putting her clothes back on. "Okay. It's your turn," Jules replied.

Landon got in and held his breath while he went under. As he came back up, he heard planes and copters flying nearby. "We have to go," Jules said, motioning him to come back. He made it back to the bank trying to put his clothes on his wet body. He threw his shirt over his head and Jules helped him pull it down. They began to move forward, moving away from the sound. "What do you think that was about?" Jules asked looking concerned. "Tracking," Landon replied. "I think they are trying to make sure they are controlling everybody and there is no one they are missing."

Staying in the direction to head to Savy's but taking a detour and feeling they would never make it; they kept moving forward. She couldn't help but look at how handsome Landon was. Even with wet hair he looked amazing. His shirt stuck to him defining the outlines of his body. He looked chiseled. Landon looked over at her and noticed that she was looking...checking him out. "You like what you see?" "What? I wasn't looking at you." "Right. Sure, you weren't," Landon laughed. "What? I was looking past you." "At what, the tree?" She gave him a 'I got caught' look smiling and rolling her eyes.

He suddenly grabbed her and pushed her behind some bushes. Jules caught her breath and they both looked beyond the brush. A helicopter landed in a field close by, and soldiers started getting out and walking around the premises. "What do you think they are doing?" Jules whispered. "We have to get as far away as we can. I will follow you to make sure no one is following us," Landon said motioning in the direction they needed to go. Jules' hands were shaking. Landon grabbed both hands and looked her in the eyes. "We can do this," Landon grabbed her face with his hands and pushed his nose against her. She felt how strong he was and knew she had to try. She was scared. Scared to get caught yet again. She just wanted to be at Savy's already. She questioned if Savy's was really even safe anymore. It was her, Landon, and God against the world.

She continued down the path to get to Savy's. Jules felt nervous and prayed as she walked.

"Dear God,

Please let us make it to Savy's. I don't know your plans in all of this, but I'm so scared. I'm trying to be strong, but I'm so tired of being strong. Please make me strong in this moment. I'm so ready to be in your presence. It's dark here and we are weary. Please help us to continue. I pray that Savy is okay. Please be with her and whoever is with her right now. I pray for strength. Amazing strength that only comes from you, and I pray you give me that to just keep going. Right now, I feel like lying down, but I'm thankful you gave me Landon. I pray that you be with Landon. Help him to know what to do in this moment. Guide us."

She never ended it with A-men. It was an open-ended prayer because Jules knew the prayer was not ending. She knew she needed Him more than ever and she would continue to pray.

Landon watched Jules as he followed behind her with his gun by his side. Looking in every direction, as He remembered from his training. Once a Marine, always a Marine. He never knew he would use his training on American soil, but America had fallen, and it was no longer the home of the free. It was controlled, and Landon didn't agree, nor would he lie down and let them have it.

Chapter 24

It was dark and cool as Kyra's dark feet slid down the mud into the water. With lanterns lighting their pathway they were determined to give their life over to whatever Jesus had for them. They had waited too long. Hanna was right behind her and held Kyra's hand tightly. They helped the little one down into the water too. All they knew was they wanted Jesus to be their Lord and Savior. Henry, Lou, Andy, Gin, Livy, Savy, and Tucker had all been baptized and were explaining to them what was to come. A new Heaven and a new Earth. It was going to be changed and this was going to be the Kingdom after this Great Tribulation they were living through. Jesus would be the

King coming back once again great and mighty. The first time He came as one of us, feeling the pain of His sacrifice He made for us, but this time He was coming looking like a mighty King. Every knee and head will bow.

Henry read as Savy held the light over Maggie's Bible.

> In Mark chapter 1 verse 4 (NKJV) John came baptizin' in the wilderness and preachin' a baptism of repentance for the remission of sins.
>
> 1 Peter 3:21 (English Standard Version) Baptism, which corresponds to this, now saves you, not as a removal of dirt from the body but as an appeal to God for a good conscience, through the resurrection of Jesus Christ,
>
> Mark 16:16 (ESV) Whoever believes and is baptized will be saved, but whoever does not believe will be condemned.
>
> Romans 6:3 (ESV) Do you not know that all of us who have been

> baptized into Christ Jesus were baptized into his death?
>
> Acts 2:38 (ESV) And Peter said to them, "Repent and be baptized every one of you in the name of Jesus Christ for the forgiveness of your sins, and you will receive the gift of the Holy Spirit."

"It is not the water that saves you. This is an act of obedience to Jesus that you will live your life for Him. You are choosin' to respond to Jesus and accept Him into your hearts."

Tucker baptized Kyra and when she came up, she opened her eyes crying and smiling all at the same time. Andy then baptized Hannah and she came up and hugged him, Kyra, and Livy. Gin, Savy, Livy, and Lou sat on the bank with their arms intertwined. It was hard for Lou to get out of the bunker and make her way to the river, but she was determined to watch more family get baptized. The lanterns shined on the ripples of the water and Sissy was baptized by Henry. When she came up, she hugged her momma and without missing a beat, Livy stepped into the water and hugged Sissy's wet pint-sized body.

They walked back to the bunker and crawled through the tunnel. They let their clothes dry out and talked about memories that they had, and things they missed and loved. Though some little chuckles filled the bunker sometimes they would pause and get quiet, knowing this life was much different now. They had so many regrets. Savy and Tucker were nestled up in the corner with one hand in the other. Gin was braiding Sissy's wet hair and Andy was holding Livy. She had grown to love Andy like a father. Henry was chuckling about the story he told of Maggie. She was running after one of the roosters because he would peck the cat on the head. The cat would hiss. This rooster caused more trouble, but he was funny and would roost in the barn up on one of the rafters and would fall asleep and then hit the ground with a big thud! It was the funniest thing. Maggie would just say, "Oh, that's ole

Roehoe." Henry laughed as he reminisced about his wife, who he missed so much.

When Kyra and Hanna's clothes were dry, they decided they needed to move on. Livy grabbed onto her new best friend and didn't want to let go. They held hands tight. Hanna bent down to the two of them. "Maybe one day y'all will see each other again. You never know God's plans." Henry gave her a Bible that they had found in an old church. Kyra looked at Hanna and smiled. "We will read this every day." She said thumbing through the pages. She closed it shut and dust came out of the pages.

On one of their journeys Henry had wanted to walk into this old, abandoned church. The boards were rotting in some areas, windows were broken out like someone had hit them with a bat, but it had been so long since he had stepped foot into a church. They went in and grabbed a few extra Bibles in case someone needed one. While Henry was there, he kneeled down at the alter in the sanctuary and cried out to the Lord. Andy was with him, and he kneeled beside him in that moment. They never told anyone about that day. They just needed a quiet place to go. They knew they could pray anywhere, but there was something sweet and reverent about that old church.

Kyra hugged Henry's neck. "Thank y'all for giving us Jesus." Henry replied, "He just used us as His messengers. It was Jesus that moved in this little bunker." "May He be with you on your journey and remember to pray for safety as you walk, please. There is so much out there. Are you sure you have to go?" Gin asked. "Yes, we would love for you all to stay with us and we all remain together," Savy responded. "We need to move forward to see if any of my relatives are still here. I can't imagine them not receiving Christ after all this time. I know now and I have to go tell them," Kyra said. Hannah hugged their necks and thanked them for all their kindness. Livy gave Sissy her plastic elephant. "Here, I've always thought this was funny looking and maybe you will think of me when you look at it. It's called an elephant.

My Mateo gave it to me and told me these animals were in zoos." Sissy hugged her and kissed her cheek. "I love you Livy." "I love you, Sissy."

They gave their last hugs and good-byes and walked through the tunnel.

Chapter 25

The whole bunker was asleep and Savy shook Tucker awake. She woke up hearing knocking at the door. Tucker grabbed his gun and whispered for everyone to wake up. Leroy jumped up waiting and watching Tucker's next move. Henry and Andy followed suit and waited as Tucker asked, "Who is it?" "It's Jules!" she cried. Savy jumped to her feet feeling her heart race. Tucker put his hand up, telling her to wait until he really knew it was her. He opened the door and looked through the crack and saw her with a man. Savy peaked out and saw her standing there tattered and tired. "Who is this with you?" Tucker asked trying to be safe and make sure this was a good idea.

"This is Landon. He saved my life," Jules said quickly. Tucker opened the door and Savy grabbed up Jules in tears. They held on to each other like their lives depended on this moment. They had been away from each other for several years. "How did you find us?" Savy asked relieved. "The house looked abandoned, and I knew you said there was storage under the barn. I'm sorry, I lost most of what I was bringing to you." "Are you kidding? Jules, all I care about is that you are here now!" Savy responded. "You look like you need some rest." "I'm exhausted," Jules said looking back at Landon. He was quiet just trying to take it all in. He too looked tired. He sat his things down feeling relieved that they had actually made it.

Jules was lying down with Savy sitting beside her. "There has to be a story with this guy. You need to tell me," Savy insisted. "He doesn't look too bad," Savy said laughing. Jules mustered a smile and led Savy on a bit. "Well...at first it was not a good situation..." "What happened? You need to tell me everything!" "Savy, we have been through some rough stuff just trying to get here. It has been so hard. I was captured and..." "He saved you," Savy whispered, but it wasn't her softest voice. "Well, he did. But this was the second time that I saw him."

"Wait! How is your grandfather?" Savy asked forgetting that this was the main reason she stayed back. "There is so much to catch up on," Jules replied. Giving a sigh, with her eyes welling up with tears, she continued. "He passed away. I knew I had to leave him. I tried to pack food and things I thought we would need. I was in the woods, and I came across Landon and Tate. Landon, at the time, was drunk. I think he was just out of it from losing everything and just trying to drink the pain away. Apparently, I had a lasting effect," Jules said, wiping the tears out of her eyes, laughing. "What did you do?" Savy said, chuckling. "Wait, why do you think it was me?" "'Cause I know you! You probably put them in their place." "Well, I did," Jules responded bluntly.

She glanced over at Landon smiling. He glanced at her and held his gaze on her for a good amount of time. He felt passion rise up inside of him. He loved her to the core of his being. "Thank you, God," he whispered out loud. Tucker went over and sat beside him. "Are you okay?" he asked. "Yes, just relieved," he said, still holding his gaze on her for a moment—then realizing and pulling his attention away and looking at Tucker. "I can't let anything happen to her," Landon said, running his hands through his messy hair. "And we will strive to protect them. I feel the same about Savy."

Jules went on to explain to Savy how she was unsure about Landon and Tate at first because it had been so hard to even trust anyone. How there is so much evil out there and it's almost impossible to hide from it. She told her how she walked away from them, but Landon found her. She talked about being captured. "It's so bad Savy. They are putting people in camps. There are helicopters tracking people. I could see people on the other side of the fence. They were happy. They were healthy. They weren't starving like we are here on the outside."

She looked down as she continued to talk about Anna, the girl that was so scared in the camp. "She was too scared to even try to escape. It's like she was frozen in time." "Oh, my goodness, what was going through your head." "Run. I just had to run. I saw an opportunity and I took it. I knew I could go down with one shot, but something inside me, maybe the Holy Spirit, gave me the strength and I just felt the urge to run," Jules stopped and looked at Savy.

"I don't know what I would've done. Maybe I would've froze. I pray that I would have been strong enough. I have always prayed that I would be strong enough, but this..." Savy trailed off. "God takes care of you in the moment. I literally think He moves you. It's something I can't explain. It wasn't my own strength. It was most definitely God. Like Daniel in the lion's den, like Meshach, Shadrack, and Abednego, like David and Goliath, or even as Exodus 19:4 (NKJV) reminds us, You have seen what I did to the Egyptians, and *how* I bore you on eagles' wings and brought you to Myself. This verse kept popping up in my mind. It's like He was showing me that He was going to get me through this. I was scared, but sometimes I think God works through us even in the midst of our fear and trembling." "So, who started the fire?" Savy asked.

"Landon. I didn't know it at the time, and I just kept running. He continued to run after me. Tate saved my life too." "I was going to ask you where the other guy was." "Yes, he...he sacrificed his life for mine to be saved. I think he knew how much Landon cared for me. I don't think he wanted Landon to do it at first. Landon seems to think he tried to step in to stop him from doing it." Jules started wiping her nose. "I didn't know there was anyone still out there like us. It seems there is so much evil that I didn't know good still existed." She wiped her cheek. "I think we have to be diligent about who we are trusting, and God will lead us."

Gin bent down and gave Jules some herbal tea. They dried out the leaves and petals two years ago. "Thank you," Jules said looking up at Gin with her swollen red eyes and puffy lips, from when she was hit by the soldier with the gun. She was having such a hard time holding it together. "There are demons out there," Jules said. "I know there are," Savy replied. "No, Savy, there are actual demons roaming now." "Did you see one?" "No, I buried my head into Landon, but he saw it. He accepted Christ right after seeing it. He wanted no part of that life." Savy looked with big eyes and Jules could tell she was frightened. "I felt scared, and I could feel it close to me. Landon was in shock, and he held on to me. I started praying in Jesus' name that it would flee from us. I had to hide myself from it and not let it be any part of my focus. My focus had to be on Jesus the whole time. I don't think there is much time left. How can we continue with immortal beings?"

Gin listened as she had her arms crossed and rubbed the outside of them as if she was cold. She felt shaky all over but tried not to seem so nervous about what Jules was talking about. "I prayed as I was walking here and trying to find the bunker. I prayed that no evil demon spirit would see us walking here. I have prayed over this bunker the entire time. I didn't even know if anyone would even be here," Jules said frantically, feeling the tears rise up for a third time. "This is an emotional night," Savy said, grabbing her hand and squeezing twice. Jules squeezed back and nodded her head trying to find words that she didn't even have.

Henry spoke up. "We have had a lot of prayer over this bunker and God has given me visions of angels all around us. We are livin' through the thick of evil. James 2:19 (NKJV) *says,* Even the demons believe—and tremble!" Henry started to pray.

"Dear Lord,

We come to you right now and ask that you put a hedge of protection around us. There are times when we have to leave this bunker. There are demons and evil lurkin' in these woods that we don't know about. Lord if we have to die, help us to die goin' in Your Mighty Name Jesus!"

"Yes Father," Gin spoke up.

"Help us to be strong in Your Mighty Name Jesus Christ our Lord and Savior. Help us win this race. Help us to feel Your presence and Your mighty angels around us. Lord, we pray that You help us to make all decisions with Your guidance and direction and protections as we come and go from this bunker."

"Father God, You know our troubles. You know what we need. Help us rest. Help us live only for You. Help us to focus on Your words as we leave. That Your words are written in our hearts." As Savy prayed Tucker bent down beside her and continued.

"Lord,

You are the One and Only, The Most High. We will see Your face one day. We pray that we have a place in Your kingdom. We know that we waited too late. We know now how lost we were, but we see now, and we are ready to be soldiers for You Lord. Lord from everything we have read in Scripture it seems that we have one more chance. A chance to show Your love in a world that is literally completely dark."

"I know that You are my Savior. I've accepted that. I may not know what to do, but You brought me through all of this for a reason. I believe You had to show me pure evil to find the only goodness there is Lord," Landon said unsure, but ready to stand. Jules rubbed him on the back.

"Father, we need You now more than ever to help us stand. At times we feel weak, but we pray that You help us keep going. Lord, we will keep going for You." Andy ended the prayer.

"A-men."

Chapter 26

"Savy! Savy, wake up!" Livy was shoving Savy's arm trying to wake her up. "Momma isn't here, and I'm scared," she whispered.

Gin felt the fresh air and breathed it in slowly. She needed this, to feel the wind against her skin. She longed for sunshine. Andy wrapped his arms around her waist from behind her and kissed her neck. She raised her arm to feel his bearded face nestled in her neck. They began to move forward as Andy was vetting the outside.

She woke up and asked Andy, "Walk with me. I need air and we can gather while we are out." He put his arm around her and brushed the hair out of her face.

She looked at Livy sleeping close to Savy. "We will come back before she even realizes we are gone."

The dried grass crunched under their feet as they walked. They had gotten to this old, abandoned house that was barely standing. Andy looked back at Gin. She nodded telling him to go ahead inside. They needed more supplies. "I will wait on the outside and watch as you go in." "No, you're coming with me." She listened, following him, unsure of what it would bring.

This house was once pretty and the fall of everything had brought it to rot. Boards were loose and they could feel the floor giving way. Gently feeling the give in the wood and trying to watch their step they went looking in the bathroom for medical supplies and anything that would be useful. Gin stopped and shined her flashlight on a picture hanging on the wall. She stared. This was a happy family. She looked at the picture longer than she should've, knowing she was there to gather supplies they needed, but she just couldn't release her eyes. This was what she had wanted, a family. The husband was laughing with his boy. They were holding up a big fish they had caught and had the biggest smiles on their faces. His son was so handsome. He had big, long dark eyelashes with brown eyes. His hair flipped out of his hat in the front, which reminded Gin of a frat boy in college. His skin looked dark, and his mom was in the background, pregnant and literally bare-footed. She had one arm under her belly cradling her stomach and the other around her daughter whose eyes were wide open and as blue as the sky. The pond was in the picture. As Gin stopped in time thinking about what that moment would have been like she smiled through the water that filled her eyes. She breathed in deep.

Andy seemed to notice and grabbed her hand. The laughter in that picture that Gin longed for resonated with Andy too. *The feeling of sun shining on her skin and being able to sit on the dock and put her legs in the water. Dipping her toes in and making those ripples in the water.* She thought to herself that maybe she would get that one day. *Maybe Heaven will have a feeling like what the picture made her feel. Maybe Livy would get to see what true happiness was.* She remembered a feeling of happiness that was evident in the pictures. *She was little and her mom was braiding her hair after swimming in the pool on the Fourth of July. She was eating a banana popsicle and her cousins were running around in their swim trunks trying to light sparklers on fire. She remembered the sound that was around her and how she felt that day. The dog ended up eating her popsicle, and she laughed so hard about the dog wanting that popsicle.*

She broke her thought as Andy was packing things up. She helped him put some canned goods in his bag. She grabbed a blanket off the couch and shook it out. Maybe she could get it a little clean in the creek and hang it in the bunker to dry. This house was fairly hidden, but they could tell others had been there. They began to step outside and then Andy's breath caught. He fell down losing any sense of life he had. "NOOO! NOOOOOO! Oh God please!" A man came toward her with the gun, she felt her heart beating rapidly and started to run. He ran after her along with others. *She never heard anyone while they were in there, and she looked as they were going into the house.* She thought as she continued to run, *how could I have been so irresponsible? Why was I so focused on a picture?*

Having nothing else to grab, someone grabbed her backpack that was on her back, and she felt someone pull her, dragging her back. She fought and he grabbed her mouth telling her not to scream. She looked frightened, but she realized it was Tucker and Landon. "I can't leave him." Gin pleaded with Tucker and Landon. "He is gone now Gin, and if you're not careful you will be too." They whispered and Tucker put his sights on the man that was headed in their direction. They were not sure how many men there were. He took him down, with one shot, as for the other man he wasn't so lucky. He had moved out of his sight. He couldn't find him. Tucker looked up from his gun and motioned to Landon and Gin to start moving back. They were back in the woods from the open field and were trying to move swiftly but quietly. They began hearing helicopters and picked up the pace a little more to get somewhere and hide. Gin, still upset, wasn't focused on her next decision. She was just following Tucker. *What will Manna Lou think? She isn't going to take this well. She thought the world of Andy. She would do anything for him.*

They moved closer to the bunker crawling low, trying not to be spotted. Gin felt an eerie feeling. A feeling of not just running low in the dark, but a feeling that she could touch the darkness. It felt thick. It felt icky. She felt so dark and depressed. She made it to the tunnel and dropped down low. She was filled with sadness not wanting to leave Andy there, so much so that her shoulders began to buckle, and her breath was shallow, feeling as if she was losing control of herself. Tucker grabbed her shoulders and lifted her chin up to him. Her head fell back against the tunnel, her stringy hair falling out of her bun. She looked at him with her dirty face and felt a feeling of defeat. "I know you loved him, and he loved you, but we can't go back there. Andy wouldn't want you to put your life at risk. He would want you to make smart decisions. "I can't tell Lou. Oh, I can't tell her. She...she is going to have a hard time with this Tucker," she said in a shaky voice trying to hold back her tears, but they kept coming. Landon got up and started moving. "Hey, we need to go in. We can't let anyone hear us." Tucker grabbed Gin's hand. "Come on Gin. We have to move."

Part 3 -

Nearing the End of the Tribulation

Chapter 27

As soon as they walked through the door, Livy ran up to Gin. "Momma!" she cried, hugging her. Livy could tell something was wrong. "Wait, where's Andy?" Livy looked upset. Ms. Lou, stiff, waiting for a response, like she knew what was coming. Gin was speechless. Tucker went over to Ms. Lou, and she went limp. "She feels clammy," Landon said. He caught her and laid her down. Savy quickly fumbled around in Andy's medical bag and grabbed a blood pressure cuff. She ran over to check Ms. Lou's heart rate. Her heart rate was very high, and her blood pressure read high. "I think she's having a heart attack." Savy looked up at Henry. He immediately started praying over her. She then began vomiting. Jules grabbed the five-gallon bucket. She was trying to help hold her head. They finally got her eased onto the bed.

"There was nitroglycerin in one of the bathroom cabinets. I think Andy grabbed it. I have to go back. If there is any way I could save Manna Lou..." "No way Gin, Savy said, "this is not your fault." "It is. It is my fault. We went on a walk. I needed air. I put my guard down." "How could you have even known this would've happen-ed?" Savy replied. Livy grabbed on to her momma scared for her to leave. "I have to Savy. Let me do this."

Jules was holding on to Landon. "I have to go with her Jules. She cannot go alone," Landon said to her. "I always come back for you," Landon said. She threw her arms around his neck. He looked at her and kissed her bye. Henry grabbed up Livy. She couldn't stop crying. "Livy," Gin said, cupping her face. "Listen, you have to calm down. Remember we are warriors for Christ right now. Remember we are to be different. You know how to be strong. You can't be loud." She responded shakily, as she tried to dry her tears up. "I love you more than anything on this planet but remember God first. He is the reason." She kissed her cheek, and she and Landon grabbed their backpacks slinging them over their shoulders, and started back out of the tunnel.

They were almost to the house when they started hearing footsteps. "We have to try and be fast." They could see the end of the forest and then just at the edge they began running. "He isn't there," Gin said looking at Landon. She got to the house and they slowly and quietly stepped in. She made her way to the bathroom, while Landon was checking the area Andy had been lying in to see if anything had fallen out of his pockets or backpack. Gin was frantic as she was shuffling things around in drawers and cabinets trying to find the nitroglycerin. She looked and looked. *Andy had it in his backpack,* she thought. It's nowhere to be found. "I can't find it." "It's not here either. We need to go back Gin," Landon said as he was scanning the outer lining of the woods. "I don't feel right about this Gin." "Okay, okay," she said as she bent down touching the blood marks on the floor. "Don't," Landon said. "Don't do this to yourself. Don't go there." Landon said in a whisper. He grabbed her arm and pulled her up.

They began to head back to the woods. It was hard moving in the dark. Not knowing where anyone was. Not knowing who was close. She thought about when she was a child. She was scared of the dark. That's what she felt like again. A child, frightened. Not knowing what was around the corner and wanting to pull the sheets up over her head and make this all go away. How her parents would run in to check on her when she had night terrors. This was a "for real" night terror. Darkness and evil lurking beyond the woods. She felt her own heart racing. Racing for an end in sight. She couldn't get back to the bunker quick enough. She heard a branch crack from under her feet. Gin was a few steps in front of Landon, but wait... *I don't hear his footsteps anymore.* Gin thought. She stopped for a minute and slowly turned around. All of the sudden in the middle of the dark woods everything went black.

She woke up feeling sick to her stomach and her vision was blurred but she could make out a fire. Her eyes came into focus, and she saw what she never wanted to see in her lifetime, Landon's body lying on the ground, Andy's, and others. She never wanted to see her loved ones that she had come to know, and trust, gone. She knew she was next. She began to use all her might to get her hands free. She felt inside that this life was about to be over. That she was not going to survive. So, she might as well go down fighting. Fighting for God, fighting for Livy, fighting for Andy, fighting for Lou, and fighting for herself.

There was a pungent smell in the air. She felt herself feeling the need to vomit, but she held it in. She couldn't draw any attention to herself at this moment. At times she would lay her head against the tree hoping no one would question if she was awake.

"I just slammed this against her head," he held up the butt of his gun. "I didn't want to kill her just yet. I felt she could be some use to us." She could hear their unhinged laughter as they made perverted jokes and motions. They were satanic and evil. She never wanted to be in this position. She just wanted to do what was right in her eyes. She didn't feel right taking no action. As they were focused on their perverted evil actions Gin felt herself moving into a vision. A vision that only God could have given her.

She saw what looked to be Heaven. She even felt different. It was brighter than she had ever seen. The glow of Heaven was eternal, and it came from her Savior. She didn't think it had been that long, but she saw God's face. She saw angels around her as she must've had one foot in Heaven. She felt a charge of electricity running through her body. She could see many dimensions that she wouldn't even be able to explain.

While Gin was having this vision the demons gathered around the evil men and the men began to wail as if they were in pain. They began to flee. She could feel the wind on her face as they were fleeing from this area.

Her mother looked at Jesus and then put her hand in hers and squeezed twice. "Gin, God is greater." She tried to stay focused on Jesus and her mom's face, but they began to fade, and she began to see darkness again.

She glanced over and noticed flames from the fire glistening off of a shiny object. As she struggled to get loose, she made out what the shiny object was. A zipper off of Andy's backpack. The medicine was in that bag. She knew it was. She felt her hands bleeding as she was forcing them out of the rope, tied tightly around her wrists. As she felt the rope begin to fray using the bark on the tree, her hands became free. She continued to assess the situation and acted as if they were still tied. She was fearful and scared. She was determined.

The men heard something in the distance. They gathered their things and ran after the noise. She continued to look knocked out. All but one was gone, and when she could no longer hear their feet, and their voices were in the distance, she bolted. She grabbed the axe that lay next to Landon. The man saw her move, and she hustled to throw it. As she lifted it, she felt the heaviness of the axe and felt all her muscles working together to then launch it at his chest. He was thrown down to the ground and she didn't even have time to realize that she had just killed a man. She grabbed the backpack and ran in the opposite direction toward the bunker.

Chapter 28

"Savy," whispered Gin loudly letting them know it was her outside. Jules rose to her feet. "Landon?" as Gin walked through the door; Jules stood there shocked. Gin looked at her with a look of sadness on her face. Jules started hyper-ventilating. Gin dropped her things, and her and Savy gathered around Jules. Not knowing what to say. "They caught me too. I'm not sure how I'm not dead," Gin cried, hugging her.

She then let Jules go and rummaged through the backpack. She pulled out the nitroglycerin to hand to Savy. "Gin," Savy said, looking at her, "she's gone." Her next words were, "we couldn't have known,"

Savy said grabbing her hand and leading her over to Ms. Lou. As they covered her head, Henry spoke up. "Gin, she is with our Lord now." Gin had cried so many tears her eyes felt swollen. She stood there and thanked God for sending her to them. A wise woman with lots of love in her heart. Gin thought about before they went into hiding how they all dedicated their lives over to Jesus. They were baptized in the same river that Hannah, Kyra, and Sissy were. Back then it was daytime, and the sun shined through the oak trees showing a reflection. They finished out the day doing more prep work for what was to come. Thinking back, they knew it was going to be bad, but really didn't have a clue what it was going to be like. Gin didn't know if any of them would make it till the end.

Tucker and Henry decided to go out and begin digging up the earth to lay Ms. Lou to rest. While Gin held Livy, and Jules rested, Savy began writing some of Ms. Lou's favorite scriptures. When Tucker and Henry returned from digging the grave,

Savy shared the words she had written, celebrating the lives of those they loved.

We lay to rest three members of our family. Part of the body of Christ. A woman that acted as a Proverbs 31 woman. She woke early, gathered harvest from her labor, she prepared food, worked long hours with her hands making sure we had clothes to wear. She took our little Livy as her own grandchild. We were all her family. She withstood this tribulation until it was her time to go home. A couple of Manna Lou's favorite verses were:

> Ephesians 4:26-27 (NKJV) "Be angry, and do not sin": do not let the sun go down on your wrath, nor give place to the devil.
>
> Proverbs 19:17 (NKJV) He who has pity on the poor lends to the Lord, And He will pay back what he has given.
>
> John 14:2 (NKJV) In My Father's house are many mansions; if it were not so, I would have told you. I go to prepare a place for you.

> Colossians 3:2 (NKJV) Set your mind on things above, not on things on the earth.

We lay to rest Andy, her nephew. He learned how to be that biblical father to Livy. He loved her as his own child. He was a man of God and wanted to get these last days on this earth right. He loved you Gin with his whole heart.

We lay to rest Landon. From what you tell me Jules, he was a protector. He knew how to love and that only comes from God. He had a healthy fear of God, and knew he wanted to be on the winning side of this.

We will be gathered to our people one day, and we know this is not our home. Henry will you please say a prayer before we go outside to lay Manna Lou to rest.

"Dear Lord,

You give us the very life that we breathe in. You are the most holy. We know that one day we will all be together again. Lord, in the book of Psalms you tell us that the Heavens declare Your glory.

The skies proclaim the work of your hands. You have shown us that you are with us in the darkness that we come across. That there is somethin' waitin' on us that is so much greater. We can't comprehend what is waitin' for us. Lord, we praise you for the provisions that you have made for us. We ask that you help us to continue to withstand Satan. In our Holy, gracious, almighty, Creator we pray. Amen."

As we got to our feet Henry and Tucker went out first to lay her body in the grave. Savy, Jules, Gin, and Livy followed. Henry and Tucker covered the grave, and Gin took Livy's hand and together they drew a cross in the dirt.

Chapter 29

After they buried Ms. Lou, they realized it was time for them to leave the safety of the bunker. They had used up all their supplies, all their food, all their water. It was a scary proposition to leave, but they didn't really feel they had any other choice.

They gathered what little bit they felt they needed and could carry with them. Then they followed in the brave footsteps of Kyra, Hanna, and Sissy. They were trusting God's grace and goodness to protect them in their journey, as they sought food, and prayed for safety in these times.

They were on the road and had felt completely hopeless. They had lost so much. They lost the ones they loved. They lost food, clothes, a warm area to sleep, they lost any rest they could've had. They had no water due to contamination in the rivers and creeks. The rivers turned blood red, and water was no longer drinkable. Their stomachs were gnawing with hunger. Their bodies felt weak and fragile.

Henry, Gin, Jules, Tucker, Savy, Livy, Lazy Susy, and Leroy walked for days. Leroy, sniffing out the trail and checking out everything he came close to, and Lazy Susy was dragging up the rear slowly. They managed to get further from the camps that had been set up. They had to camp in a cave and wait for soldiers to pass. The darkness helped not to be spotted as easily, but at times it worked against them as they moved. Finding a log, they stopped to give Livy and Lazy Susy a rest. Her feet hurt and she was so tired. "I don't know how much longer we can live like this," Savy whispered in Tucker's ear.

He grabbed her hand, "I don't know either, but we can't give up."

He looked into her tired eyes. Those eyes that he fell in love with looked weak and ready to give up. "Look at me," he said. "Keep going Savy." She nodded her head. Livy fell asleep. Jules was tired and heartbroken. She hadn't spoken for days and was still in shock, not knowing what the world held and so ready for this tribulation to end. How could they keep going? She just sat on the ground Indian style and held her head in her hands looking down at the ground. Savy rubbed her back, "I love you, Jules."

They decided to get away from the road for the time being, and Tucker picked Livy up cradling her. Savy watched Tucker. He was so loving. Livy's head lay against his chest and her dirty feet and legs were hanging from the bend of his arm. She was an exhausted tough little girl.

Savy thought about a time when life was softer, and kids didn't have to be so strong. It was a time when people were a little more spoiled. *Wants were simply a click away and packages were delivered to the door.* Her thoughts drifted to how young teenage girls compared themselves on social media. *They weren't pretty enough, they were too fat or too skinny, their stomach wasn't flat, they wanted to have their makeup perfect, they wanted their bodies to be desirable. The depression it often caused when they were thinking they were not good enough. Little did they know there would always be someone prettier and those standards were fake anyway.* She thought about what America used to be before the "Big Change." People had the chance to show up at church, one of them being herself, but didn't. *They cared more about their own schedules than taking time out for Jesus Christ. America, and the rest of the world, ran out of time. They felt they had plenty of time to do what they wanted, instead of asking God what He wanted.*

They raised themselves above His name and were now living with those consequences. *How were we all so vain? How did we not see that we were acting just like they did in Noah's time? Every intention was evil, wickedness had grown on the face of the earth, and it grieved God that He had even made man. The stories in the Bible of Sodom and Gomorrah or the story of the Tower of Babel seemed to be replaying themselves out in this time of tribulation. The worst of mankind. We were living in modernized sin. Why did people make things okay for themselves, instead of looking to our Savior? Having an idol. Phones were in every hand and selfies mattered*. If Savy could go back to that time, she would've tried to live differently. *She would have told that young seven-teen-year-old she didn't need all that. She would have tried to make a difference.*

"Are you okay, Savy?" Tucker asked interrupting her thoughts. "Yes, I'm just thinking about how life in America used to be." "Wishing you could go back?" "If only I could've changed how I lived then." "I would've listened to your dad," Tucker said, as he was breaking up kindling for a fire. Livy was lying on the ground on top of his jacket. A jacket that was given to him before everything happened. The jacket was from Savy's dad. He saw that Tucker had been working outside early in the morning without a jacket. The next day it was left in the tack room with a note:

Tucker put this on and keep it.

Real heartfelt I know, but the fact that he did that for Tucker put a smile on his face. He was a giving man, not great with words at times, but cared deeply for Tucker.

"I would've come home more," Savy said. Tucker stood up as the fire began to catch. He wrapped his arm around her waist. It felt warm to be next to Savy's side. His thumb rested in her belt loop. She rested her head on his shoulder. "I would've met you sooner," she said. "Oh, I saw you one day when I was out feeding. You had come home and were grabbing your suitcase out of the car. You were struggling with it, and I was headed down from the barn to help you, but your brother came out to help before I could get to you." "Wow, I think I would've noticed those eyes," Savy said.

Her hands started to shake. Tucker noticed she was not feeling good. He grabbed his pack and gave her a sip of water. Then he put in one small container of salt and shook it up a little bit and gave her some. "Not too much," Savy said. "We need to save it for everyone else." "Right now, you need this to be here for us," Tucker said. She drank a little of the salty water.

Henry slept leaning against a tree with his gun in his arms. Everyone was exhausted and felt they had no reason to live. They rested and listened to the frogs and crickets. They had tried to give it their all, but at this moment they had to stop and lay down. Henry hadn't felt well. His legs had been going numb throughout their journey.

Tucker looked around seeing that everyone he loved was at their end. The darkness weighed heavily on their attitudes and their thoughts. He was always leery to fall asleep first. He felt the need to be a watchful eye. Making sure they were safe and that anything the darkness held would flee and not try to lurk around them. There were shadows and noises, and Tucker knew that the spiritual world on the dark side was working overtime. He had to keep focused on God, because it was so easy to fall into the darkness and be depressed. He focused on Savy and his tribulation family who he loved. He and Savy made a point to give their love to Livy and help raise her.

Suddenly there was a brightness in the sky. It was like a radiance they had never seen. They all began to get up off the ground one by one and make their way back to the road. When they came to an opening through the forest, they saw a radiance that illuminated the whole sky*. It was happening. Savy realized, just like the letter from her mother, and the scripture we have read about as a family, it was time. It was Him!* The Holy of Holy's on a white horse in the sky. The clouds rolled back like a sea in the sky. The darkness over the whole earth vanished.

We began to feel a warrior-like presence over us and knew that He had won. King Jesus stood in glorious victory. We stood in awe. This was the start of the Millennial Kingdom. We would serve Him. There was a large army behind him on horseback. His army filled the sky, and generations of people were on God's side. Angels of all kinds were surrounding the army. The blasts of a trumpet sounded, and we all began raising our hands up in praise. Tears of joy filled our eyes, and a feeling came over us that was amazing. The Holy Spirit made our hearts passionate.

Savy felt her breath leave her body, but it felt good and refreshing. It was a new feeling she had never felt before. Her body began to float and all she saw was a glowing gold that magnified of light. She came into focus and there stood a horse just for her. Her dad was standing there with the horse. There were no reigns. He just listened and stood. Her dad was smiling, and she hugged him immediately.

Holding on to the happiness that filled her heart, she saw her mom and other family members already on the backs of their horses and they were ready for battle.

> Revelation 7:13-14 (NKJV) Then one of the elders answered, saying to me, "Who are these arrayed in white robes, and where did they come from?" And I said to him, "Sir, you know." So, he said to me, "These are the ones who come out of the great tribulation, and washed their robes and made them white in the blood of the Lamb."

> Revelation 7:16-17 (NKJV) "They shall neither hunger anymore nor thirst anymore; the sun shall not strike them, nor any heat; for the Lamb who is in the midst of the throne will shepherd them and lead them to living fountains of waters. And God will wipe away every tear from their eyes."

The Lord and his horse looked giant and radiant. When he turned to look at everyone, all the horses bowed in reverence. Everyone reached their arms towards The Lord. He looked over at us and an angel blew a trumpet and He shouted, "Well done good and faithful servants." Savy mounted her horse and then began. They rode into battle, and the Lord took care of the evil on the earth. A feeling of rest, relief, happiness, comfort, and love radiated in each of the Lord's servants.

A bright city high above everything in the sky. It was beautiful and breathtaking. They couldn't remove their eyes from it. It looked like the brightness of a golden jewel and clear as crystal. The feeling of a great wind came over them. They heard a mighty voice say:

"It is done! I am the Alpha and Omega, the Beginning, and the End. I will give of the fountain of water of life freely to him who thirsts. He who overcomes shall inherit all things, and I will be his God and he shall be My son."

The city on this huge mountain began descending. We couldn't take our eyes off of it and no one said anything. We were just in complete awe. A moment that we had all been waiting for. The new Jerusalem.

Savy looked around in awe of the beauty that surrounded her. Her mother ran to her and hugged her. Her family surrounded her. She saw Tucker and her family from earth. They were happy and she noticed they were not gaunt looking. Henry was with Maggie! Ms. Lou gathered with her family. Gin and Andy were laughing with Livy, as she reached to pet that huge, majestic lion. Jules was in awe and had fallen on her face kneeling in great respect and reverence for our Father Jesus Christ. Savy followed, bowing before her King.

Before they knew it, everyone was bowing. They heard singing and a feeling that could not be explained by the human mind. A sound that was so wonderful to her ears. She could understand all languages being spoken. She saw people that were recognizable, and she was happy to see them. A bowl was laid before the people that had just come out of the great tribulation, at the feet of our Lord. This bowl was the prayer of the saints. "Lord! You are Holy!" She heard the saints begin to sing. It was the sound of eternal prayer.

Gift of Salvation

Prayer, faith, salvation, and hope are important and given freely from God through Jesus Christ. If you have not yet accepted Him, or want to renew your faith and commitment, I would love to hear from you. If you have read this book and it has helped in leading you to Christ, please reach out to me.

This is a work of fiction, but it is very real in scripture and the prophecy that God gives us. He is coming quickly.

Please use these scriptures when prompted by the Holy Spirit to guide someone in the Roman Road to Salvation.

Romans 3:23 (NKJV) For all have sinned and fall short of the glory of God,

Romans 5:8 (NKJV) But God demonstrates His own love towards us, in that while we were still sinners, Christ died for us.

Romans 6:23 (NKJV) For the wages of sin *is* death, but the gift of God *is* eternal life in Christ Jesus our Lord.

Romans 10:9-10 (NKJV) If you confess with your mouth the Lord Jesus and believe in your heart that God has raised Him from the dead, you will be saved. For with the heart one believes unto righteousness, and with the mouth confession is made unto salvation.

Romans 10:13 (NKJV) For, "whoever calls on the name of the LORD shall be saved."

If you would like to give yourself over to Jesus Christ as your Lord and Savior allow me to lead you in this prayer.

Dear Lord,

I know that I am a sinner. I know that I am not able to save myself. I believe that when you gave your life on the cross, you paid my debt completely. Forgive me for the sin in my life and take your rightful place as my personal Lord and Savior.

A-Men.

About the Author

Skye Burgdorf is busy with home-schooling her children, working as a hair stylist, and helping her husband with the youth ministry at church. She came to know Jesus as her Lord and Savior at a young age and has a passion for studying Bible prophecy. She enjoys going to the beach, the quietness of country living, and spending time with her family. Skye resides near Leiper's Fork, Tennessee, with her husband and two children.

Follow Skye on Facebook:

www.facebook.com/profile.php?id=100087508596072

Follow Skye on Instagram! Username: skyeburgdorf
www.instagram.com/skyeburgdorf?igshid=ZDdkNTZiNTM=

Email Skye at: SkyeBurgdorf@mail.com

Skye Burgdorf

To follow Skye on Instagram:

To leave a review or order more books (for bulk orders contact Skye):

If you loved the book, Savy thought you may enjoy the book trailer! Open it in Facebook and share it with friends so they can learn about and read the book too!

Skye Burgdorf

Connect on Instagram:

Printed in Great Britain
by Amazon